"During that trial, I watched you and you watched me...."

He lowered his voice. "I see you're shaking your head in denial. But it's true. Day after day, we got to know each other a little better."

"That's absurd!"

But Luke kept on talking. "I realized from the start that I'd been framed and would probably lose the case, so I found myself fantasizing about you. About what it would be like to talk to you, hold you, touch you. About what happened when you welcomed me into your arms with a kiss any man would die for."

Andrea gasped at his words. Could he read her mind? He had just described her own feelings, her own reactions. But she didn't dare admit that. "I think prison has distorted your perception of what went on," she said instead.

"On the contrary, it clarified many things for me."

"What do you want, Mr. Hastings?"

"Luke. And you know exactly what I want, Andrea."

Rebecca Winters, an American writer and mother of four, is a graduate of the University of Utah. She has also studied at schools in Switzerland and France, including the Sorbonne. Rebecca is currently teaching French and Spanish to junior high school students. Despite her busy schedule, Rebecca always finds time to write. She's already researching the background for her next Harlequin Romance!

Books by Rebecca Winters

HERO ON THE LOOSE
Rebecca Winters

Harlequin Books

TORONTO • NEW YORK • LONDON
AMSTERDAM • PARIS • SYDNEY • HAMBURG
STOCKHOLM • ATHENS • TOKYO • MILAN
MADRID • WARSAW • BUDAPEST • AUCKLAND

ISBN 0-373-03265-X

Harlequin Romance first edition May 1993

HERO ON THE LOOSE

CHAPTER ONE

"ALL RISE," the sheriff called out as Andrea Meyers, the last of the twelve jurors, filed into the courtroom. Her eyes, more purple than blue, quickly sought out the defendant, seated next to his attorney. The jury had been deliberating for more than four hours, since the verdict had to be unanimous for a conviction. Those hours must have felt more like years to the man whose future was about to be determined.

Although the circumstantial evidence proved he was guilty beyond a reasonable doubt, Andrea hadn't received that confirmation in her heart. Maybe she had difficulty coming to a guilty verdict because she was an ordained pastor and disliked being anyone's judge. Her reservations, which had no basis in tangible evidence or proof, had delayed the proceedings by a couple of hours, frustrating the other jurors.

"Everyone be seated!" The white-haired judge turned in his chair. "Has the jury reached a verdict?"

The spokesman rose to his feet. "Yes, Your Honor. We have."

Again, Andrea found herself studying the defendant as she had frequently throughout the ten-day trial. His tall well-built body, his air of authority and power, made him stand out from the other people in the courtroom. Lustrous dark brown hair was brushed from a side part to frame an aristocratic face with a straight nose and well-defined jaw. In his middle thirties, he was the personification of the high-bred Wall Street type, impeccably dressed in an expensive-looking navy suit. Andrea suspected that if he was ever to smile, he would be one of the handsomest men she'd ever seen.

"We find the defendant, Lucas Hastings, guilty as charged."

A soulful cry from a smartly dressed brunette standing at the back of the room reached Andrea's ears the instant before pandemonium broke loose. Andrea hadn't seen her since the first day of the trial. The accused wasn't married, but Andrea assumed the attractive woman was a close friend. If Andrea had been in the woman's place, she also might have found the trial too painful to sit through day after day.

The judge pounded his gavel. "Order in the courtroom." When there was silence he said, "Mr. Hastings, we'll continue your bail and you'll be released on that bail until your sentencing. Or you can waive the time and have sentencing pronounced now."

The defendant's wiry red-haired attorney jumped to his feet. "We would like time before the sentencing and would suggest a date six weeks from—"

But he wasn't allowed to finish his statement, because his client pulled on his arm and engaged him in private conversation.

The attorney stared at his client in bafflement, then turned to address the judge. "Your Honor, my client desires to have sentencing pronounced now."

"Very well. Mr. Hastings, you and your attorney, Mr. Rich, will approach the bench and stand before me."

Unable to look away, Andrea watched as a mask seemed to slip down over the defendant's face, leaving it expressionless. He rose smoothly to his feet, betraying no hint of anxiety or stress. How could a person who'd been convicted of a serious felony appear so aggressively self-assured—even defiant—at a time like this?

With a dignity Andrea couldn't help but admire, he stood before the judge, his hands clasped in front of him and his dark head erect.

"Mr. Hastings, prior to my passing sentence, do you have anything you would like to say at this time?"

"I can only reiterate what I've said all along. I'm not guilty, and one day I hope to prove it."

His deep, clear, unwavering voice resonated throughout the courtroom, but it was his simple declaration of innocence that troubled Andrea.

None of the other jurors had had any difficulty finding him guilty, and her reservations before casting the final vote hadn't caused them to reconsider their decision. So why was she still agonizing? Why did the nagging conviction persist that he could be innocent despite the overwhelming evidence?

Because you were once accused of something you didn't do, Andrea Meyers. No one had believed her, either, and the consequences had been heartbreaking.

As ghastly as that episode had been, she'd managed to put it behind her and get on with her life. But this trial had resurrected those feelings of helplessness and hopelessness with painful clarity. Was Lucas Hastings suffering in the same way?

The judge had ordered the jury to find him guilty only if guilt could be determined beyond a reasonable doubt. Andrea followed his instructions to the letter, dissecting the evidence to find even one tiny snag in the whole damning scenario. The fact that she couldn't turn up anything concrete in his defense eventually forced her to vote with the others. But she couldn't help wondering somewhere deep in her heart if the district attorney's case was just a little too pat, a little too perfect.

Sometimes the damaging evidence didn't tell the whole story. And sometimes it told the wrong story altogether.

Worried by her doubts, which had their roots in the far-distant past, Andrea prayed she'd done the just thing where the defendant was concerned. The problem was that a guilty verdict hadn't *felt* right, and it felt even less right now.

She glanced surreptitiously at the other jurors to see if any of them were struggling with last-minute doubts. But from the stoic expression on each face, she guessed they were all of exactly the same opinion as they'd been during their deliberations.

"Mr. Hastings," the judge began, "I'm compelled to remind you that in your trusted position as part owner of a stockbrokerage as prestigious and success-ful as Hastings, Radley and Fyans, the crime of fraud and embezzlement hurts the image of all financial in-stitutions in whom society at large puts its trust.

"I find no excuse for your behavior and therefore sentence you to five years at the federal prison in Red

Bluff, but place you on probation after six months, contingent on your good behavior, because you've already returned the money from your private assets. I now remand you to the custody of the sheriff.''

Just hearing the word "prison" made Andrea's stomach clench in dread. The thought of spending even one day behind bars, let alone six months, horrified her. If she could be grateful for one thing, it was that he would be sent to a minimum-security prison.

According to Paul Yates, the senior pastor at her church who occasionally conducted religious services there, Red Bluff was a federal "camp" facility that catered to white-collar criminals like Lucas Hastings—high-profile men who'd been convicted of tax evasion or fraudulent schemes and needed protection from the more-dangerous felons housed in maximum-security prisons.

At least he'd be spared the horror of serving time with hard-core killers. Somehow Andrea couldn't imagine him confined in such a place, even if he *had* broken the law.

In her preoccupation, she hadn't realized she was staring at the defendant. It came as a jolt to discover that his dark bitter gaze, which had been trained on the judge, was suddenly focused on her. Many times throughout the trial she had caught him staring at her. Just as often, their eyes met in long unsmiling communication and she had been able to gauge his mood by their expression, which changed from probing or watchful to speculative, even assessing.

But this time she shivered. For one brief moment, she thought she detected a glint of confusion and unguarded pain mingled with that defiant angry look.

Then his attorney pulled him aside, breaking the contact. Again she found herself wondering if there had been a gross miscarriage of justice, and an innocent man was going to prison.

Distressed by her reaction, she turned to confide her feelings to one of her fellow jurors. But to her surprise, they had already left the courtroom, eager to get back to their jobs and families. Jury duty disrupted lives, yet it was the process by which the country's legal system functioned.

Andrea cast a fleeting glance at Lucas Hastings and winced as she watched the sheriff put him in handcuffs. It seemed the height of absurdity to restrain him, to treat him like some powerful half-wild animal that had suddenly turned dangerous. Tight-lipped, he strode from the courtroom with his head held high, as if what was going on around him wasn't really touching him.

A group of people, including his business partners who had professed to care for him and seemed visibly shaken by the painful proceedings, tried to follow him. But the attorney held them back. He took a moment, though, to console the distraught woman who had run down the aisle of the courtroom only to be ignored by the defendant.

Tears sprang to Andrea's eyes and a deep sadness entered her soul. Talk about lives being disrupted! In the space of a few seconds, a man's whole world had been destroyed, irreparably hurting the people who were closest to him, as well.

Andrea knew what that was like. Eight years before, she and her fiancé, Mark—the one person she had come to rely on—had been driving to the church for their wedding rehearsal when a semitrailer veered across the median and crashed into them.

In mere seconds, her world had collapsed. Mark didn't survive. Andrea shouldn't have lived, either, and for months afterward, she wished she hadn't. But in time she came to view her survival as miraculous. In fact, when she contemplated her life, she saw that it had been full of miraculous reversals. That recognition had eventually led to her life's work.

Surprised by where her thoughts had wandered, she gave herself a mental shake and hurried out of the courtroom to the parking lot. She had been away from everything for ten days now and was anxious to get back to the heavy demands of her schedule; she'd inevitably fallen behind in her paperwork. Work was the only cure for lingering doubts like hers.

But her mind wouldn't stop replaying the events of the trial, particularly the damaging testimony of Lucas Hastings's business partners. Throughout the ordeal they appeared reluctant to give the evidence that ultimately put their friend behind bars.

More than once, she'd entertained the possibility that his associates had framed him and in fact had been playing roles, fooling everyone with brilliant cover-up performances. Something similar had happened to her years before, and the one person who knew the truth, the person who had created the nightmare in the first place, had baldly lied, leaving her nowhere to turn.

When Andrea raised this possibility to the other jurors, they had dismissed the notion on the assumption that neither of Hastings's partners would dare risk the penalty of perjuring himself. She'd had to admit they were probably right. If the defense attorney hadn't found anything suspect about his client's partners and their testimony, then who was she to say differently?

One thing was certain. She never intended to serve on a jury again. If she was called for future duty, she would exempt herself on the basis of extreme bias *for* the defendant. She would explain that the nature of her vocation caused her to believe in humanity's basic goodness, and that, more often than not, she made decisions based on instinct and intuition.

Lucas Hastings's destiny had been put in the hands of his jurors. For Andrea, it had been the most painful duty she had ever been forced to discharge. She didn't think she could bear to shoulder that kind of responsibility more than once in her lifetime.

A warm June breeze disheveled her shoulder-length black hair as she got into her compact car and drove from the city center toward the modern southwestern-style church with its beamed cathedral ceiling. Ten minutes later she hurried into Paul's office, anxious to discuss her concerns with him. He was her mentor, and if anyone could help her, he could. He had a way of putting life into perspective.

The instant he saw her sweep into his office, he greeted her with a hug and urged her to sit down. Though separated in age by almost forty years, Andrea felt a strong rapport with the burly widower. She looked upon Paul as she might have done a father. She hadn't known either of her parents. Nor, for that matter, had she ever known anyone as compassionate and strong of character as Paul. She loved and admired him, and he returned her feelings. His only son,

Brett, worked in Japan, and Paul clearly thought of Andrea as his second child.

"I take it the trial is finally over. Why so troubled?" he asked at once. "Where's that sunny smile of yours?"

"The man is going to prison, Paul."

His expression sobered. "Do you want to talk about it?"

She nodded as tears moistened her eyes. "Mine was one of the twelve votes that sent him there."

After a reflective moment Paul said, "And now you're suffering over your decision. Didn't the verdict have to be unanimous?"

"Yes, of course."

"Then it means that all the other jurors found him guilty, as well."

"That's true." She wiped her eyes with a tissue from his desk. "But I can't help worrying that it's possible we've sent him to prison for a crime he didn't commit."

The older pastor sat forward in his chair. "I'm not surprised you'd say that. You often let your heart lead." Raising one hand, he said, "Please don't take offense. It's a godly virtue and an endearing trait. The world would be a far better place with more of your kind in it."

Andrea shook her head, half smiling. "Nothing you say could possibly offend me." Paul was a diplomat, but she knew the truth about herself. In her teens she'd been accused of something terrible she didn't do. Such a traumatic experience had left scars, and since that time she more often than not found herself championing the underdog, allowing her emotions to take over. She was well aware that this tendency could flaw her ability to judge people and situations accurately.

Andrea sighed deeply. "You've touched on the very thing that's been bothering me," she went on. "I was the only holdout when all the other jurors considered it an open-and-shut case."

"That's because you didn't *want* to find him guilty."

"I don't know, Paul. It's far more complex than just wishful thinking. During the trial, something didn't add up, something I could never put my finger on." She stirred restlessly. "What if he's innocent?"

"Then it would be a tragedy. But the sad truth is he wouldn't be the first man to spend time in prison for a crime he didn't commit. However, even if that's true, there's nothing to be done now."

"But what about him? If you'd been in that courtroom and heard him say he was innocent, it would have shaken you, too."

"I have no doubt of it. But the reality is he was found guilty by all of you because of the evidence against him. Therefore it's reasonable to assume you didn't make a mistake. Remember, too, that it's human nature for most people like the defendant to deny involvement when they've been accused of a crime. False pride has a lot to answer for, and no one is infallible. Not him, not me, not you."

"You're right, of course," she whispered.

"I wish I could help, but it appears your dilemma will have to be solved by time and prayer. You're burdening yourself unduly with something that's out of your hands."

"I know."

"Andrea—" he looked her squarely in the eye "—go home and relax. Do something frivolous. That's what I used to tell my Constance when she was a little blue. More often than not she took my advice and came home hours later with a new dress or pair of shoes, and a fresh outlook."

Andrea got out of her seat and hurried around the desk to give him another hug. "Thanks for the talk and the advice. Now I can go home. See you later, Paul."

After leaving the church she headed for the apartment she leased in a less-affluent residential area of Albuquerque. Perhaps one day, if she continued to build her savings account, she'd be able to buy a little house of her own. But that time was a few years away yet.

As she pulled up to the curb, she could see her landlady, Mabel Jones, in the front yard, surrounded by several flats of petunias. That meant Andrea wouldn't be able to slip inside the house without first facing a barrage of questions. The middle-aged widow was understandably lonely but enjoyed gossip, something Andrea tried her best to avoid.

Right now she felt drained and wished she'd been more observant, because she didn't feel like talking to anyone, least of all a curious Mabel. However, Mabel had seen her and it was too late to drive off again. Andrea couldn't risk offending the woman, who not only provided her with a large and comfortable ground-floor apartment at low rent, but was a stalwart member of the parish's church council.

Unable to throw off her depressed mood, Andrea got out of the car and prepared to deal with Mabel, who came running up to her, trowel in hand, several gray-brown hairs escaping her loosely fastened chignon.

"Is it over, Pastor, or are you home to freshen up before you have to go back?"

"It's over, and I'm exhausted."

"When I think that several members of our congregation have trusted Lucas Hastings's company to handle their investments, I shudder."

Somewhat impatiently Andrea murmured, "Their money's still safe. As you read in the newspapers, he paid back every dime by liquidating his assets. No one lost anything."

But her defense of Lucas Hastings went right over Mabel's head. The woman persisted, saying, "It's indecent how much money the man's worth, let alone that he's such a handsome devil. You can't trust his type, because he's above earning a living like common, ordinary folks. All he's after is to get rich quick off other people's hard-earned savings. To my way of thinking, it's out-and-out gambling, and all stockbrokers should be investigated. I hope he got everything coming to him. Tell me what happened," she finished avidly.

Andrea took a calming breath, still haunted by the look in Lucas Hastings's eyes before he was escorted from the courtroom in handcuffs. "He was sentenced to prison for six months. You'll hear all about it on the six o'clock news."

The older woman's brows knit together, making her look cross. "Only six months?" she wailed, obviously bursting to discuss the case in minute detail. But by this time Andrea had reached the front porch and started to open the door.

"That's right. Please forgive me if I don't stay and talk. I need to have lunch and get ready for work. If you'll leave some of the petunias on the porch, I'll plant them in the morning. They're just beautiful, Mabel. They'll make the garden look wonderful."

Only slightly mollified, the older woman sniffed and mumbled something in reply as Andrea disappeared into the house.

She tried to eat a sandwich, but a feeling of weakness came over her and she lay down on the bed to rest. She got up an hour later, unrefreshed, because thoughts of Lucas Hastings had kept her tossing and turning. Determined to get her mind off the trial, she showered, changed into fresh clothes and drove to the church once more. Since her induction to jury duty, Paul had been handling her responsibilities along with his own and it was time to relieve him. The thought of going shopping, as he'd suggested, held no appeal, but hard work might help her forget her worries.

When she arrived at the church, she discovered that Paul had gone into town to attend a YMCA meeting and would probably be away the rest of the afternoon. That was fine with Andrea, since it meant she could plunge into the mound of paperwork sitting on her desk without Paul's urging her to go home. She dealt with a dozen phone calls needing to be returned, then started in on the staggering amount of mail. When she finally checked her watch, two hours had passed.

"Doris? Would you come here for a minute, please?" she called to the church receptionist. Andrea got up to stand in front of a glass-framed scripture on the wall that she frequently used for a mirror. Beneath the three-piece white-and-yellow seersucker suit, she fastened the white collar she wore for official church business. A flick of the brush through her dark hair and she was ready. Other than a coral-frost lipstick, she didn't wear makeup. Her heavily lashed, pansy blue eyes needed no artifice.

"You don't have to tell me," Doris said as she entered the office. "You're off on your hospital rounds. Why don't you give tonight a miss? After more than a week of jury duty, I know I'd be dead on my feet."

Andrea's hand was unsteady as she put the brush back into her purse. "The trial upset me a great deal. I'd rather keep busy so I won't think about it."

"If you ever feel like discussing it, I'm here to listen," Doris murmured compassionately.

"One day I may take you up on that, Doris." And it was the truth. If ever she could bring herself to talk to anyone about what had happened at the trial, Doris would be that person. "But right now I'm on my way to Barbara Montgomery's. Her mother's been diagnosed with cancer and just arrived from South Dakota. Barbara's going to take care of her now. She asked me to drop by. Apparently her mother's pretty depressed and scared of undergoing chemotherapy." She paused. "I think Barbara's scared, too."

"A visit from Pastor Andy is exactly what they need."

Andrea smiled warmly at the attractive blond mother of three who wasn't much older than her own thirty years and had been her friend from their first meeting. Not everyone in the parish had accepted Andrea after her ordination two years ago. Some never would. But she'd learned to handle rejection and not let it interfere with attaining her goals.

Closing the distance between them, she gave Doris a fierce hug. "Thanks, friend."

Doris gazed fondly at Andrea. "You've got a lot of them, don't forget. If there are some who still haven't found out you're pure gold, then they're the ones with the problem."

"Well, I was certainly blessed when you applied for the secretarial position." Andrea gathered her briefcase and purse. "The choir is practicing now. Will you remind Tom to lock up when he leaves? I don't want you staying here until they've finished, or you'll be late picking up your kids. You don't get paid enough as it is, and I won't have you putting in overtime, particularly on a Friday night."

"Hey, it's all right. Greg's out of town until next Wednesday." Doris smiled. "Mom doesn't mind."

"Well, I do!" Andrea spoke in a firm voice.

Doris cocked her head to the side. "And what about you? All work and no play. You know what they..."

"I like my work. I love what I do."

"And what about the other kind of love? The man-woman kind?"

Andrea's mouth curved in a smile of amusement; Doris never gave up. "You tell me."

"I happen to know two men who've started coming to Sunday worship because they're crazy about you, but you look right through them. That's not very charitable of you," she teased.

Andrea paused on her way out the door. "I know who you mean, and I like them both. But to be honest, neither of them appeals to me in a man-woman way," she said. "Besides, you know the church frowns on the clergy becoming romantically involved with one of their own parishioners. Not to mention," she added wryly, "that it would scandalize Mr. and Mrs. Sloan, and we can't have that."

"The Sloans don't live in the real world and they don't speak for the whole parish, Andy."

"You could've fooled me." The Margo Sloans of the world were dangerous, and no one knew it better than Andrea.

Doris moved closer. "Forget them, and tell me this. If you met someone who really attracted you, you wouldn't turn him down, would you?"

In that instant, an unbidden image of Lucas Hastings flashed through her mind. Disturbed because he still dominated her thoughts, Andrea said, "Let's put it this way. If I ever meet a man who can make me forget Mark, then maybe. Now get that matchmaking look out of your eyes. I have to go. See you Sunday."

Twenty minutes later Andrea parked her car in front of a high-rise apartment building near the downtown area. Once inside, she pressed Barbara Montgomery's buzzer and was allowed admittance. She took the elevator to the fifth floor.

Her visit lasted more than two hours. Mostly she listened and hugged Zina, Barbara's mother, who cried a great deal and confided her fears and frustrations. Andrea suggested she might enjoy participating in a support group Andrea had started for adults who were battling any number of emotional, psychological or physical problems. They met at Andrea's place every other Sunday night. Sometimes they watched instructional videos on overcoming obstacles or listened to motivational guest speakers. Occasionally they did community-service projects together.

Andrea's idea was met with a great deal of enthusiasm on Barbara's part, but getting a commitment from Zina was more difficult. Andrea gently suggested that maybe Zina would meet someone there whose fears were even greater than her own. Perhaps they could be of comfort to each other.

Zina blinked and after a brief hesitation said she would think about it. Barbara sent Andrea a look of heartfelt gratitude before seeing her to the door. "Thank you, Pastor," she whispered.

"Anytime, Barbara."

Oddly enough, the minute she got into her car, her mind insisted on again conjuring up images of Lucas Hastings to the exclusion of all else. What were his feelings as he faced his first night in prison? Even if he was guilty, the prospect of sleeping in a locked cell for months on end had to be daunting. And what if he was innocent, as he claimed?

Andrea didn't want to think about that and on the drive home made an effort to concentrate on the sermon she would deliver Sunday morning. In a way, she'd been preparing it her whole life. "Judge not, lest ye be judged." As far as Andrea was concerned, only a higher power could know the true intent of a person's heart.

Again her thoughts centered on the man whose unforgettable face had filled her vision for the past ten days. How would he spend all those weeks and months confined to a cell after being the dynamic force behind a thriving brokerage house?

Throughout the trial, the defense had painted pictures of a man with incredible energy and talent. A man who was a genius with figures, a man who had come from a moneyed background. Why would such a person want or need to commit fraud? Simple greed?

Andrea concurred with the judge, who said he found no excuse for Lucas Hastings's behavior. But she went further than that. She found no *reason* for such behavior, no motive. Somehow that part had never made sense to her, despite the facts presented to the contrary, and she supposed his guilt or innocence would always remain a mystery.

But as Paul said, it was over, and there was nothing more to be done. She'd performed her duty as a citizen and now the best thing to do was relegate the trial and Lucas Hastings to the past. Wasting any more time worrying about him would be nonproductive.

She served a parish that needed all her attention and concern. It would be best to concentrate her energies there, where her efforts could bear fruit.

CHAPTER TWO

THE SEPTEMBER COMMITTEE meeting to plan the church's year-long calendar of activities finally drew to a close, with several important problems still to be solved.

"Can I have a private word with you?" Paul asked as Andrea rose to her feet.

She nodded, and once everyone else had left, propped herself on the corner of his desk. "I know what you're going to say, and I'm as concerned about Ray's transfer as you are. Who do you think we can get to coach the kids in team sports after he leaves? The boss at his new company wants him in California right after Thanksgiving. That doesn't give us a lot of time to find a replacement of his caliber."

Paul shook his head. "I don't know. Maybe we'll have to advertise for volunteers from the community. Or better yet, maybe some of the high school students know a coach who would be willing to lend us a hand one evening a week. But don't worry. We'll find someone. We always do. In the meantime Richie Green is willing to fill in until we get a permanent replacement. But that's not the reason I detained you."

He sat forward in the chair, his eyes glowing, and Andrea could sense an air of excitement about him.

"How can you look so happy when we've got the weight of the world on our shoulders?" she teased.

"I had a letter from Brett. He and Susan want me to fly to Tokyo for a visit and see the children. They sent me a round-trip ticket."

"That's wonderful!" Andrea cried. "You deserve a vacation more than anyone else I know. When are you going?"

"*If* I go, it'll be two weeks from today, and I'll be gone for two weeks."

"What do you mean, *if?*"

He patted her hand. "I don't like leaving you when we've got the problem of a shifting foundation and an inept building contractor."

Andrea's smile faded. "Is that your polite way of telling me you don't think I'm capable of handling things without you?"

"You know better than that," he said in a gruff voice. "I guess what I'm saying is that I feel guilty about going off to have so much fun while you're left alone to deal with everything here."

"How do you think I felt when I was on jury duty and you had to cover for me for ten days? Now I can pay you back."

"You're sure?"

She grinned. "Start packing your bags. I'll take care of the rest." She got up from the desk. "Why don't you go home right now and phone Brett with the good news? It's about time those children got to know their wonderful grandpa."

His eyes misted over. "Thank you, Andy. I think I'll do just that."

The next two weeks flew by as they made arrangements and worked things out so he could leave. Before long, Andrea was driving him to the airport, and en route they discussed last-minute church business. When she pulled up to the entryway, Paul turned to her.

"I'm sure I've told you this, but in case you've forgotten, it's written on the calendar I left for you. Next Sunday afternoon is our turn to hold Communion and deliver the sermon at Red Bluff prison. Since they require a thorough security check before entering, I've already phoned in the necessary information and you'll be given clearance at the visitors' office as long as you have your driver's license."

She blinked. *Red Bluff?* That was where Lucas Hastings was serving time. For the last couple of months Andrea had managed to put him and the trial out of her mind. "I don't know, Paul. I've never conducted services at a prison before."

He chuckled and reached for his camera bag. "You have to do it sometime. Just remember, it's a church service like any other."

When she thought about facing a group of male inmates, she started to panic. "Did you leave the talk you prepared so I can study it before Sunday?"

"Since when do you and I deliver each other's sermons? That's your department. I leave it all in your more than capable hands." At that point he got out of the car, opened the back door and pulled out his suitcase. "Don't bother to come in. It'll be at least an hour before my flight."

"But, Paul—"

"Goodbye, my dear Andrea, and many thanks for the ride and the homemade candy. I'm going to take your advice and have the time of my life. With you in charge, I have no worries. God bless you. I'll see you in two weeks."

She watched his large figure lumber toward the airline terminal and disappear into the crowd. Naturally she was excited for him, but as she drove away from the airport, she couldn't help wishing he were leaving a week later so she wouldn't have to go out to the prison. There was a possibility that Lucas Hastings would be in the congregation. The idea of delivering a sermon with him there unnerved her more than a little.

She supposed she could call someone at the Shared Ministry Council and try to arrange for a minister from another church to go give a sermon, instead. But that idea didn't sit well because she'd never been one to shirk her duty. Besides, she knew Paul was depending on her and would be disappointed if he learned she'd bowed out because she feared the challenge.

When she really thought about it, she realized Paul had paid her a supreme compliment by expecting her to go in his place—particularly since more often than not, it was male clergy who visited the men's prison. It meant Paul had full confidence in her abilities. She couldn't let him down.

The rest of the week she spent interviewing contractors until she found one she thought she could trust to give her some honest answers and a decent bid for renovations. Then she juggled her work load so she could prepare a meaningful sermon for the prison service. But every once in a while thoughts of Lucas Hastings crept in to distract her.

The judge had told him he'd be let out of prison after six months, contingent on good behavior. Was he a churchgoer? She remembered Paul's telling her that only a small percentage of inmates took advantage of church meetings, and so she figured the chance of Lucas Hastings being in the congregation was too remote to worry about.

Still ... what if she did see him assembled with the others? Would he recognize her as one of the jurors who had condemned him to prison? She knew she'd never forget *his* face. However, it had been almost three months since that dreadful day, and he probably wouldn't connect a female pastor dressed in Communion robes with one of the three women who'd sat on his jury. After all, she hadn't even worn her collar.

By Sunday, she felt reasonably comfortable with her decision to take Paul's place, and as soon as morning services at her own church concluded, she ate a quick lunch and started out for Red Bluff, a hamlet approximately eighty miles east of Albuquerque. During the drive, she rehearsed the words she would say at the pulpit and hoped they'd have meaning for the prisoners and provide encouragement.

The one-story prison had no fence and didn't look as intimidating as she'd imagined. The guard at the visitors' office checked her identity before escorting her to the small interdenominational chapel on the main floor.

As they approached the doors, she could hear men's voices raised in song. Paul had told her the inmates had formed their own choir. When she and the guard stepped inside the chapel, a dozen or so inmates dressed in military khaki pants and matching short-sleeved shirts were practicing around a piano.

Her arrival caused some curious stares as the guard led her to a sterile cubicle off to one side of the chapel where she could change. He explained that the tiny windowless room, containing only a table and two chairs, was used for conferences between inmates and clergy.

After he left, closing the door behind him, she opened her suitcase. First she put on her white Communion robe. Then she removed the other things she'd need for her service and hurried into the chapel to make preparations.

A glance at her watch told her it was almost two o'clock. Placing a folding chair at the back of the chapel next to the door—where a different guard was now posted—she arranged copies of her sermon, plus some other material that she'd photocopied at the church. The men could pick up the reading material as they left after the service.

On the rectangular table at the front of the chapel near the raised pulpit, she set out everything she needed for worship. Then she introduced herself to the choir and pianist and asked them to open and close the service with hymns.

They agreed, eyeing her with open interest. Except for visiting hours, she supposed a female at the prison was a rare sight, particularly a female pastor.

At two on the dot, she watched twenty or so men of various ages file into the chapel and take their places on the folding chairs. She would know Lucas Hastings anywhere, and his face wasn't among them.

Breathing a sigh of relief, she nodded to the choir and they began to sing. Soon the service was under way and she was able to relax. After prayers and Communion, she noticed that the guard allowed a few latecomers to enter the chapel and sit in the back row to hear her sermon.

It wasn't until halfway through her talk, explaining to the inmates how small acts of kindness could be performed right here in the prison, that she saw the man she had helped put behind bars. No other inmate had those striking features and that lustrous brown hair....

For a brief moment her voice faltered and she fought to pull herself together. Purposely staring at the front row in an effort to concentrate, she concluded her sermon. "Remember that when you're free to reenter society, those acts of kindness can be enlarged to include volunteer work to people less fortunate than yourselves. The world is full of so many needs, there's a place for all of you to serve, in any capacity you choose. I've left some material concerning community service on the back chair if you'd care to take it with you as you leave."

After she gave the benediction, the choir broke into song and one by one the inmates left the chapel, Lucas Hastings with them. Obviously he'd noticed nothing out of the ordinary, and Andrea felt a surge of relief.

Several inmates approached to shake her hand and thank her for the message. One teary-eyed man of about twenty hung back, and when the room emptied asked if he could have a private word with her. He'd already cleared it with the guard.

She urged him to come into the adjoining room where he broke down sobbing. He begged Andrea to contact his mother and tell her he was trying to change and hoped she could forgive him one day. Apparently the letters he wrote always came back unopened.

Andrea's heart went out to the young man, and she wrote down the woman's address, promising she'd write to her and convey his feelings. He thanked Andrea profusely, then left. She took off her communion robe, anxious to get back to Albuquerque. It had been a long day in more ways than one, and the nervous strain she'd been under had taken its toll—especially once she'd seen Lucas Hastings seated among the others.

But when she turned to go into the chapel to collect her other things, the object of her thoughts blocked the entryway. She came to a halt hardly daring to breathe.

"Pastor Meyers?" His distinctive voice—a voice she would never forget—broke the quiet. "If we might have a word?"

Andrea could only stare at him. She had never seen him in anything but conservative business suits, immaculately groomed, and wasn't prepared for the sight of him in the close-fitting prison pants and shirt—clothes that revealed his well-defined chest and muscular legs.

She found the clean natural scent clinging to his lean body rather stimulating. The shadow of beard covering his firm jaw and the skin above his upper lip added to his raw appeal. Her gaze wandered to his hair, which was longer now; it curled around his forehead and neck in rakish disarray.

He, in turn, made a study of her slender figure and long elegant legs. Slowly his admiring gaze traveled over the full curves visible beneath the white linen dress and navy blazer she wore, sending hot and cold chills through her body.

But the moment his assessing gray eyes moved to her clerical collar and finally came to rest on her flushed face, they narrowed, turning black as ebony. Instantly his handsome features hardened into the sober mask she had seen when the judge pronounced sentence.

"It *is* you," he whispered with icy disdain.

He'd recognized her, after all. Weaving slightly, she took a step backward, stumbling into one of the chairs. "Mr. Hastings" was all she could manage before his mouth twisted in mockery.

"During that farce of a trial I noticed every exquisite detail about you, but I don't recall the collar. Am I to assume that while I've been serving time as a felon, you received your badge of sainthood?"

After what he had just said to her, she struggled for breath *and* her wits. "I was ordained a pastor more than two years ago, but I wouldn't have worn my collar for jury duty, because I wasn't on church business."

His dark brow furrowed menacingly. "Perhaps you should have. It might have entitled you to divine inspiration. Lord knows, it was needed," he murmured in a bleak voice. He folded his arms, drawing her attention to their corded strength and to the dusting of hair on his upper chest.

"What brings you to New Mexico's most celebrated country club? Did you decide to go slumming

today, hoping to see how the infamous other half
lives?''

She fought to remain calm. "The Shared Ministry
conducts interdenominational services here on a
weekly basis, and today was my turn to deliver the
sermon.''

His gaze wandered insolently over her face and
body, setting every nerve ending on fire. "Well, if it's
a larger number of converts you're after, sending you
to a prison full of men who'd probably kill for the
mere sight of a woman was a stroke of genius. I'm
surprised there aren't signs of mass rebellion already.''

Andrea hadn't anticipated talking to Lucas Hastings and was taken aback by this particular kind of
harassment. Within seconds he had penetrated her
defenses and gotten beneath her skin, leaving her
feeling exposed and vulnerable.

Shifting her weight, she found herself explaining,
"Actually, I'm here in Paul Yates's place. He's the
senior pastor at my church, but he's out of the country.''

He flung back his head and angry laughter filled the
reception area. The guard, who had now stationed
himself outside the tiny room, turned quickly in their
direction, but Lucas Hastings appeared oblivious.

"I'm afraid you're not a very convincing liar—since
you're the very first female pastor to step inside these
walls, while I've been here, anyway. Now why don't
we practice a little honesty? You heard the sentence
pronounced at my trial, so you knew I was locked up
here. Should I be flattered you decided to pay a visit,
to survey the damage, so to speak? Were you hoping

to find out I'm still alive, to salve your conscience in some twisted way? If I don't miss my guess, this must be an unpalatable first for you, rubbing shoulders with the notorious convict you helped send to prison."

"You have an inflated sense of your own importance, Mr. Hastings," she retorted. "Yes, I knew you were here and thought it a remote possibility you might show up at services. But my motive for coming was to help some of the inmates draw closer to God and find a little solace."

"There's about as much chance of that happening in here as of you becoming Pope!"

Though she was feeling weak-kneed, Andrea stood her ground. "There are times in a person's life when he needs comfort from a higher source." While she spoke, his eyes studied her mouth, giving her the impression he wasn't concentrating on her words.

"The platitudes roll so easily from those proper lips it's hard to believe you weren't born wearing a collar. Let's get something straight, *Pastor,*" he emphasized with derision. "If there was a God, I sure as hell wouldn't be in here!"

Until her early twenties, Andrea remembered thinking the very same thing, particularly after awakening in a strange hospital room unable to move. But the hostile man confronting her wouldn't be interested in hearing about her past. In fact, she couldn't envision a time when Lucas Hastings would listen to *anything* she had to say.

He muttered an imprecation that caused her body to tauten. "What? No sermon? No diatribe on my godless condition?"

"Would it do any good?" She flung the question at him and immediately regretted it.

"You know damn well it wouldn't!" he exploded.

"Then why did you come to the service?"

"To give further evidence of my good behavior. Why else?"

Knowing she was in over her head, she said, "If you'll excuse me, Mr. Hastings, I have to gather up my things in the chapel."

"What's the matter?" he taunted. "Afraid to be alone with a real live convict?"

"I've never thought of you as a convict."

His eyes flashed dangerously. "So you admit you *have* thought of me."

"I wouldn't imagine any of the jurors have forgotten your case. It isn't every day—"

"You send an innocent man to prison?" he asked roughly before she could finish. Andrea's eyes closed for a brief moment. He was still maintaining his innocence. His declaration disturbed her even more acutely than it had in the courtroom three months earlier.

"The jury did its best to weigh every piece of evidence."

"And that's supposed to make me feel better?" He moved closer, but she was too mesmerized to back away. "What's this all about?" His undisguised bitterness shattered what little composure she had left. She felt a desperate regret that she hadn't found someone else to come out to the prison in her place.

"Look, Mr. Hastings, whether you believe it or not, I suffered a great deal of anguish over your case and—"

"Of course you did," he broke in curtly. "All of four hours, to my recollection."

"You didn't give me a chance to finish," she reminded him, but wasn't allowed to go on because he unexpectedly grasped her chin in his hand, lifting her face for a more thorough scrutiny. Every thought fled from her mind as she felt the pressure of his fingers against her hot skin. His nearness only served to confuse her, and all she could think about was his unsmiling mouth, inches from hers.

"Tell me something, Pastor," he whispered silkily, making her title sound repulsive. "Have you ever known a moment's unpleasantness, let alone had your soul thrust into hell? Felt your life shaken to its very foundations? Has anything so profound ever caused this lovely facade to crumple in hopeless despair?"

Locked in an agonizing battle, Andrea wanted to tell him yes, she *had* been there, probably more times than he could imagine, but for some reason her mouth refused to work. Maybe it was because of the haunted expression on his face, which had gone white from the force of his emotions.

"Has it?" he demanded. In the next instant his other hand gripped her upper arm and he shook her. She knew the gesture was unconscious on his part, that he was using her as an outlet to vent his anger. But the guard in the doorway was on the alert for any sign of trouble and she saw his hand move to his holster.

Immediately Andrea divined the outcome and realized it was up to her to avert disaster. Because of their precarious situation, she had unwittingly provoked Lucas Hastings to the point of rage, but the guard would only see the other man's response as an act of violence.

She refused to allow him to suffer any more pain because of her unintentional interference. Improvising fast, she cried, loud enough for the guard to hear, "Luke, darling! I know you told me not to come, but I couldn't stay away!" On that impassioned note she pressed her mouth to his, wrapping her arms around his neck, hoping to fool the guard in the most convincing way possible. She could only pray Lucas Hastings had caught on and wouldn't push her away.

She needn't have worried. Almost at once she felt his hands slide beneath her blazer to splay across her back and draw her fully against his hard body. Andrea's slight gasp of surprise allowed him to deepen the kiss she had initiated.

Afraid not to cooperate, she found herself being kissed so thoroughly she was in danger of forgetting where she was or why she'd come. What was more, the taste of his mouth, the slight rasp of his unshaven jaw, sent a thrill of excitement through her body. Shocked by the liberties he had taken and by her own response to them, Andrea tore her lips from his and peered at the guard through her lashes. To her satisfaction, their heated embrace had checked his movements. He stood outside the doorway, watching them with interest.

Limp with relief and other emotions less easy to identify, she tried without success to move out of Lucas Hastings's powerful arms. "You can let me go now," she said in a cracked whisper.

A low devilish laugh came out of his throat. "No way," he whispered back, forcing her to look into his dark, fathomless eyes. "Not yet." For a fleeting moment Andrea could well imagine him guilty of every charge brought against him and more. "Not until you tell me why you went to such elaborate lengths to see me in the first place, and why you were willing to turn yourself into a human shield to protect me from the guard."

"I've already told you. I came in Paul's place because he asked me to," she murmured, still incoherent. Not only were there too many conflicting emotions tearing her apart, she was unbearably aware of his thighs brushing hers, his heartbeat resonating against her palms through the cotton shirt. Gritting her teeth, she said, "Now I'm not so sure it was a good idea."

His wry smile taunted her. "Did I shock you by taking advantage of what you offered? Did you forget I'm a man, as well as a felon? One, furthermore, who's been deprived of a woman for quite a while now? You must admit you served yourself up on a silver platter." He chuckled, then added, "I have to admit that the second I breathed in your perfume and felt your mouth against mine, I forgot all about your collar and started imagining you without any...embellishments."

"How do you dare speak to me like that?" she demanded in a strangled voice, hazily aware that she was in trouble.

"I dare because you threw yourself at me." His chuckle became positively demonic. Before she could think how it had happened, his mouth was covering hers again, this time in a slow, seductive kiss that went on and on, draining all the fight out of her. She tried disciplining herself to remain rigid and unresponsive, but he only laughed at her futile attempt to dampen his ardor.

Worst of all, desire began licking through her body of its own accord, something that had never happened before, not even with Mark. She fought him, but not nearly hard enough. The feel of his mouth, the sensations she was experiencing, left her captivated, as though without will or choice.

When she finally did pull away, he nuzzled the tender skin of her neck with his jaw, then murmured against her ear, "Have you suddenly decided I'm not worth saving, after all, not even in the name of your precious God? All you have to do is tell the guard what's really going on. He'll make sure I'm not around to terrorize any more hapless female pastors foolish enough to wander into the devil's territory."

As if the guard knew he was being talked about, he called from the doorway, "Time's up, Hastings! Back to your cell!"

Andrea could hardly believe it when he let her go. Seconds later she felt her face grasped between a pair of strong hands and lifted to his enigmatic gaze.

"Thanks for the visit. Maybe our meeting like this *wasn't* your intention. Nevertheless you've given me something to dream about. How about one more for the road?"

Without asking permission he lowered his head and pressed his mouth to hers. A low moan escaped her throat, and he smiled knowingly as he lifted his head and traced her trembling lower lip with his thumb. "My feelings exactly. Now get out of here. Go on home where you'll be safe from big bad wolves like me.'' His piratical grin was the last thing she saw before he disappeared from the room at a run.

The incident left her feeling so fragmented she grabbed hold of a chair to steady herself. When she could function again, she hurried into the adjoining room, put her things in the suitcase and left the chapel.

Andrea didn't remember anything about her flight past the visitors' office to her car or the trip back to Albuquerque. All she knew was that she'd trespassed where she shouldn't have and been warned off in a way that mortified her every time she thought about it. Lucas Hastings was a convicted felon in what the other jurors saw as an open-and-shut case. Today his behavior made Andrea feel she'd voted the right way, after all.

Why she hadn't detected the lawless, arrogant, untamed side of his nature in the courtroom was a question that would probably remain unanswered. But at least she'd never have to see him again. Forgetting him meant putting the whole experience behind her and never discussing what happened at Red Bluff with a living soul, not even Paul. Eventually the incident would fade from her memory.

In the meantime, she intended to change the way she approached life. From now on, Paul wouldn't be able to say she let her heart rule her head. Those days were over.

CHAPTER THREE

"I HATE TO TELL YOU, Andy, but you have to hit the ball like *this* if we're ever going to win a game!" Richie demonstrated his prowess at the volleyball net in the church gymnasium while the other members of the team—all teenagers—looked on.

"Maybe you guys should stay in front, and Lisa and I'll cover the back," Andrea retorted good-naturedly, flashing a conspiratorial smile at the shy high school girl who was having every bit as much trouble as Andrea was returning the opposition's powerful serve.

Richie was taking his role as temporary coach and captain seriously. Andrea tried to follow his directions, but every time the ball came her way, her well-intentioned hit went awry. Volleyball had never been her strong suit, but she was determined to master the sport if it killed her.

The interdenominational Youth Council coed volleyball championships were coming up at the end of February, which was less than two months away. To make this year's competition more exciting, the western district superintendent had established a new rule that a member of the clergy of each parish had to join the team. Since Paul's doctor wouldn't have allowed him to indulge in such vigorous activity, the honor automatically went to Andrea. She'd groaned in dismay at the prospect, but there was no way out of it.

After smoothing a few tendrils of hair that had escaped the braid she'd pinned to the top of her head, she planted herself inside the foul line the way Richie had taught her and waited. When one of the serves headed in her direction, she prepared to volley it forward and high. To her horror, she sent the ball sailing backward in a perfect arc.

The kids on both sides of the net burst into laughter and Richie collapsed in despair, bringing their practice game to a screeching halt. He lay facedown, kicking his legs and pounding his fists in mock anger against the newly waxed floor.

Flushed from exertion and embarrassment, Andrea smoothed the pale pink running shorts over her hips. Like everyone else's white practice jerseys, her top clung to her body, faithfully following the outline of her curves. "I know I've got a lot to learn, Richie Green, but I'm not *that* bad."

"That's a matter of opinion," Matt Carranza teased before dazzling her with the smile that had won him the title "Best-looking Hunk" at the local high school.

"Thanks for the vote of confidence, Matt," Andrea muttered. "The next time you want a big favor from me, just remember what happened here today." But she winked as she said it, then ran to the back of the court to retrieve the ball.

As she bent to pick it up, she heard a man's mocking comment from the doorway. "Actually, the kids have a point."

Her hands froze on the ball.

She knew that voice.

It could belong to only one man. A man whom, three months ago, she'd sworn to forget. A man whom she'd hoped and expected never to see again. *When was he released from prison and how did he know where to find me?* she wondered.

Panic sent adrenaline flooding through her system. When she finally lifted her head, her stunned gaze collided with Lucas Hastings's probing glance. A sudden paralysis attacked her body.

Like a Technicolor movie, memories of their last meeting played through her mind, suffusing her already heated face with dark red splotches.

He was propped against the door looking larger than life, clean-shaven and dressed in white jeans and a navy sweatshirt. She was forcefully reminded of the virile picture he had presented in the tiny room off the prison chapel. After submitting her to another frank appraisal, a satisfied gleam entered his eyes. "It's nice to know you haven't forgotten me. As you've no doubt discovered, certain experiences can never be obliterated from the mind."

She thought she'd already suffered the ultimate humiliation at his hands that day in the prison, but such wasn't the case, it seemed. He obviously found perverse pleasure in reminding her of an encounter she had tried unsuccessfully to forget, an encounter that revealed the very human side of her nature. He knew she'd lost her head the moment he'd touched her, and apparently it provided him no end of delight.

Dazed by his wholly unexpected presence, she rose to her feet, the ball forgotten. She started to tell him that he wasn't welcome at the church and had no business coming near her. But her words were wasted because he'd already plucked the ball from the floor and had headed toward the teenagers grouped around the volleyball net.

"What do you think you're doing?" she yelled, running after him. He ignored her.

"Hi, kids. My name is Lucas Hastings, but my friends call me Luke." For a disturbing moment his eyes met Andrea's furious gaze, sending her a pointed message that reminded her of that moment at the prison when she'd cried, "Luke, darling!" The mere recollection bathed her body in another wave of heat.

"The Reverend Yates told me you lost your coach after Thanksgiving. Since I used to play a lot of volleyball in college, I decided to volunteer as a replacement."

Andrea thought she must be dreaming. But the kids seemed oblivious to her turmoil, clearly thrilled to have this attractive, athletic-looking man for their coach. In fact, she was astounded at how easily he commanded their attention.

They clapped and cheered and asked him a dozen questions at once. Did he know the championship games started next month? Did he know any good moves to ace out their competitors? Would he be able to hold as many practices as they needed? Would he teach Pastor Meyers how to hit the ball properly?

The last question sent everyone into gales of laughter, and they all turned to see her reaction. But Andrea was still recovering from her initial shock at seeing him again. While one part of her felt a shivery excitement she couldn't suppress, another part was appalled by his brazen appearance in her private domain.

Why didn't Paul discuss any of this with me?

Anxious to question the senior pastor, she left the gym quickly, conscious of Lucas Hastings's eyes following the movement of her long bare legs as she disappeared through the double doors.

Paul was in the chapel pointing out the faulty heating vents to the furnace people. The moment he saw her, he excused himself and ambled to the area in back of the pews where she stood.

"What's wrong, Andy? You look upset."

"I am, actually. Lucas Hastings breezed into the gym a few minutes ago and announced he was the new coach. I'd forgotten he'd be out of prison by now. Furthermore, I had no idea you'd ever met him. How and when did all this take place? I would have expected you to talk it over with me before you asked him to coach the team," she said, trying to calm down.

"Let's go to my office where we can talk in private." After telling the workmen he'd be back, he ushered her down the hall. Andrea couldn't remember a time when she'd been upset with Paul, but Lucas Hastings's presence in the gym had completely thrown her.

Paul shut the door. "Why don't you sit down?"

"I couldn't," she said as her chest rose and fell with the strength of her emotions.

He perched on the edge of his desk and stared at her, his expression puzzled. "I first laid eyes on the man a half hour ago."

Andrea blinked. "You're kidding."

"No." He shook his gray head solemnly. "As I understand it, he called the church on Thursday wanting information and Doris told him we worked here on

Saturdays. So he came to my office and asked if he could talk to me. No one was more surprised than I when he told me his name.''

"I don't believe it," she muttered more to herself than him, hugging her arms to her waist.

"He simply told me that last week he was released from prison and wanted something useful to do with his spare time. He was carrying the tract you handed out the day you delivered your sermon at the prison.'' Her mind reeled at the revelation. *So that was how he found me.* "He said your talk about doing volunteer work made a real impact on him."

"But that's impossible," she thought aloud, remembering the outrageous way he had spoken to her, his irreverence for everything sacred.

"Apparently not," Paul continued, still unaware of the chaotic state of her emotions. "It seems you were the instrument used to help him."

"No." She shook her head. Paul was giving her credit for something that was patently untrue. Any minute now she would have to confess the truth.

"Don't be so modest." He reached out to squeeze her shoulder. "Of course, I was delighted with his request and told him we had dozens of projects requiring volunteers. When we went over the list, he said he felt best suited to helping out in our sports department." His smile widened. "With the competition just around the corner, he's the answer to our prayers, Andy. After I told him you were all in the gym practicing, he said there was no better time to start than right now."

Andrea didn't know what to think and looked away, trying to come to grips with the fact that in one mas-

ter move, Lucas Hastings had well and truly en-
sconced himself in her life. She simply couldn't take
it in.

"I thought because of your concern over him at the
trial, you'd be pleased to know that he was now a free
man. The only reason I didn't consult you first was
because I wanted to surprise you with the actual fruit
of your labors. I'm proud of you, Andy. In one prison
visit, you managed to make a difference where he was
concerned."

"Oh, Paul." She broke down and started to unbur-
den herself. Within a few minutes she had told him
everything except for certain intimate details that still
had the power to make her blush scarlet. "Perhaps
now you understand why I'm so disturbed. I can't believe he's here to help anyone, and I don't trust his
motives. In fact, I don't trust him, period, and think
it unwise to allow him to work with the team.

"Let's be honest," she went on. "He's an ex-convict
and the antithesis of the kind of role model we want
for our youth. If I'd asked the council to find another
person to go out to the prison that day, we wouldn't be
in this predicament now. It's my fault, and I'll take the
responsibility of telling him we've changed our minds
and don't want him to work here."

A long silence ensued before Paul said anything at
all. "You know, I thought I'd lived long enough that
nothing could surprise me, but you've managed to do
it. Andy, why are you taking this position now?
What's changed your mind? I know he was rough on
you in the prison, but after all he's been through, did
you really expect him to welcome you, one of his jurors, with open arms?"

She bowed her head, unable to respond; too many feelings were at war inside her.

"Whether innocent or guilty, he's paid his debt to society and must live with the taint of a prison record for the rest of his life. Would you crush him underfoot when he's at his lowest?"

"Of course not. I simply don't want to have any dealings with him." What Andrea refrained from saying was that she didn't trust *herself* around him. He'd aroused the passionate side of her nature and it frightened her.

"That doesn't sound like the Andy I know and love. He's one of God's children, too, and he needs help."

"Paul, Betsy Sloan is on the team. What will happen when her parents find out we recruited an ex-con as coach? You know there'll be trouble. And you should hear Mabel Jones on the subject. Mark my words, when the news is out, you can plan on half your team not showing up."

"That's why I urged Mr. Hastings to sit down with the kids and tell them the truth before he did anything else. Let *them* make the decision. I trust their judgment."

"It's not the youth I'm worried about. They're the first to defend the underdog. Besides, he had them eating out of his hand from the moment he made an appearance in the gym."

"He has a definite . . . presence."

Andrea would rather have died than admit Paul was right. "I don't suppose he told you that he doesn't believe in God."

Paul shook his head. "The subject didn't come up. However, I'm not nearly as concerned about what a man says as what he does. Be honest, Andy. Not only did you meet him under difficult circumstances, but you yourself know through personal experience that things aren't always what they seem.''

She shuddered because his admonition struck close to home. "All I know is that I made a grave mistake when I went to the prison in your place, and now I'm paying the price. If you don't mind, I'm going home. Whatever's happening in the gym, it's just as well if I'm not there. I'll see you in the morning, and I look forward to hearing your sermon.'' She patted his arm. ''I'm sorry to be such a disappointment to you. Right now I'm not too happy with myself, and...and I need some time alone to think.''

Before he could say anything else, she left his office and headed for hers to put on long pants and a parka more suitable for the cold January day. She waved to the workmen on her way out the side door. A jade green BMW convertible parked in the lot between Paul's Chrysler and the men's work van was impossible to miss.

Not every ex-convict drove away from prison in such splendor. As Andrea started up her economy car and pulled into the traffic, Mabel's castigations about wealthy stockbrokers came to mind. By tomorrow the parish would be agog with the news, and Mabel would haunt Andrea's door, wanting to know all the juicy details.

Groaning at the realization, Andrea stopped for a hamburger, then headed out of town for a few hours' aimless driving, needing the distraction before she went home to endure a sleepless night. After the trial it had taken her several weeks to stop actively thinking about him. And after her visit to the prison three months ago, she'd suffered more insomnia. Now it was going to start all over again and she knew of no antidote short of requesting a transfer to a parish in another state. Even then, it would be a long time, if ever, before she had real peace of mind.

Mabel had called him a devil, albeit a handsome one. Andrea decided the appellation fit, since he obviously had a propensity for causing trouble. Now that he was out of prison, with an unlimited source of income and no job to keep that razor-sharp brain of his occupied, what better way to pass the time and amuse himself than by harassing her—the person foolish enough to confront him in prison.

She felt her face go hot with the memory of the sensations his mouth had aroused and her own passionate response. Gripping the steering wheel tightly, she turned her car around and drove toward home.

But by the time she'd reached her neighborhood, she grudgingly acknowledged that the man had to be at loose ends and needed something like coaching to fill the hours while he put his life back together.

As soon as she arrived at her apartment, she showered and got ready for bed. Then she sat down at her desk and worked on the first drafts of enough spiritual messages to supply the church newsletter for the next six months. She wrote until three in the morning, at which point the pen slipped from her fingers, the first sign that she might actually be able to get some sleep before having to face a busy Sunday.

ANDREA COULDN'T REMEMBER the last time she'd been late getting to church, but since the appearance of Lucas Hastings in her well-ordered life, nothing seemed to be the same anymore. She felt emotionally and spiritually out of tune, something that hadn't happened since long before she had made the decision to become an ordained minister.

Junior choir started at eight-thirty, followed by youth classes at nine-fifteen. Sunday worship began at ten-thirty. Normally she arrived at the church around seven to open the library for the teachers, answer the phone and make sure everything would run smoothly for the day.

But on this particular morning, it was quarter to ten before she pulled into the crowded parking lot and dashed into the church. Everything seemed to be under control, which shouldn't have surprised her because Paul would have seen to any emergencies.

She felt like a sneak, hurrying down the back hall to her office in the hope that no one would see her. After locking the door, she slipped on her Communion robe, then headed for the foyer of the church to help Paul greet the congregation.

He had started the custom of visiting with his parishioners on Sunday mornings years ago. When Andrea, fresh from the theological seminary in Oakland, California, was assigned to serve as his associate pastor in Albuquerque, New Mexico, they'd continued the practice. She'd always looked to him for guidance and applauded his methods of drawing closer to the people he served.

Preparatory to the start of services, members of the adult choir had already donned their robes and were gathering in the hall. As Andrea greeted each of them, the familiar sounds of a Bach fugue filled the church.

She hurried to take her place opposite Paul at the front doors.

Though he was busy carrying on a conversation with a newly married couple who had moved into the parish, he managed to wink at her. His private signal let her know he understood why she was late and that there was nothing to forgive. She loved him for it.

Now that it was January, people were back from Christmas vacation and the foyer began to fill quickly. Andrea hugged many of her parishioners, who were like family to her, inquired after their health and asked about any good news she could share with the congregation. She shook hands with newcomers and urged them to ask questions and take home any pamphlets or brochures available on the rack in the front hall.

"Zina!" she exclaimed in surprise when she turned to welcome the next in line and discovered Barbara and her mother standing there.

"Good morning, Pastor," the older woman said in a quiet voice. "I've had a pretty good week and wonder if it's all right if I come to your house for the meeting tonight."

Pleased that Zina was at last exhibiting interest in joining the support group, she said, "It's more than all right. I'll be looking forward to seeing you. Seven o'clock."

"We'll be there," Barbara assured her.

As soon as they moved on, Andrea automatically put out her hand to greet the next person—and saw it swallowed by Lucas Hastings's firm grip. To her chagrin, Margo Sloan stood directly behind him.

In some tiny corner of her brain she'd wondered if he might appear. Once again she found herself his prisoner, as the warmth of the contact sent shock waves of pleasure through her body. No doubt he could sense her reaction and the realization humiliated her even further—particularly with Margo Sloan watching every move they made.

Of course, the older woman could have no idea of the dangerous undercurrents between them. Fearfully Andrea lifted her gaze and saw the mocking challenge in his.

"Do you think lightning will strike me if I tell you how lovely you look this morning in your ecclesiastical robes?" he murmured.

At her slight gasp, his lips twitched and he tugged on her hand, drawing her that little bit closer. "It's no wonder the men couldn't stop talking about you. You were wise not to show up at the prison again. Those incredible violet eyes alone would have incited a riot." Though he had spoken quietly, she didn't put it past him to create a scene and wondered how she could get rid of him.

Panicking, she said something that was totally out of character for her. "Six months behind bars hasn't curbed your tendency to take risks that could easily land you another prison sentence."

A low chuckle followed and the pressure on her hand increased. His disarming grin made nonsense of her threat. And worse, it allowed her a further glimpse of his potent sex appeal, making her heart turn over in spite of her suspicions that he was up to no good.

"I don't believe that any man, ex-convict or otherwise, has ever been arrested for complimenting a beautiful woman. Even if she is a pastor." While he spoke, his thumb idly caressed her palm. To her horror, his touch sent darts of awareness through her body; worse, she was sure Margo Sloan could tell exactly what was happening.

"You're holding up the line," Andrea muttered through clenched jaws. "Services are ready to begin. Has prison life robbed you of all decency?"

She tried to pull her hand out of his without letting Margo or anyone else notice, but the attempt was futile.

"I'll release you on one condition."

By now her cheeks were on fire. "You're despicable."

"Do you want to hear it?" he whispered, the question clearly a warning.

Too upset to form words, she met his bold stare and let her icy gaze speak for her.

"We have unfinished business. I'll come by your place tonight."

"No!" she said sharply. "I'm busy this evening."

"Lisa Jennings told me all about the group that meets at your house every other Sunday night. I'm planning to attend. Until then, Pastor."

He let go of her hand and walked with infuriating nonchalance into the church as Andrea reeled from their unexpected encounter. She had no doubt he meant what he'd said and would show up at her apartment that evening. The fact that he knew she didn't want him there must have made him all the more determined. And thanks to his conversation with Lisa, he was confident of his welcome, because the meeting was free to anyone who wished to come.

Trust Lucas Hastings to draw out the shyest, quietest teenager in the group. Without Lisa's being aware of it, he had elicited the information he wanted while at the same time making the girl feel singularly important. It just went to prove how dangerous he was.

"Good morning, Pastor." Margo's brittle voice broke into Andrea's disturbed thoughts. She wanted to rail against such an injustice. The accusation in the older woman's gaze seemed to cut Andrea to shreds, and she geared herself for an attack.

"Mrs. Sloan. How are you this morning?"

"I was planning to have a word with the Reverend Yates about his irresponsibility in hiring an ex-convict to coach the children. But after what I've just seen, I should have guessed he didn't come to such an imprudent decision by himself."

Andrea had the overwhelming urge to tell Margo Sloan the truth—that far from encouraging Paul, she had almost jeopardized her relationship with the senior pastor over the matter of Lucas Hastings. But she wisely refrained. The other woman had never been able to accept Andrea in a ministerial role and had made it her personal mission to broadcast Andrea's slightest flaws to the rest of the parish.

"If you're concerned," said Andrea tightly, "then please take it up with the church council. Talk to Hal Neff if you wish to call a meeting—he's the new chairman." She stopped talking when she realized Paul was making his way to the front of the church. "Excuse me, please. The service is about to begin."

Without waiting for a reply, Andrea hurried inside and took her place behind the choir members who had begun walking down the center aisle, pacing themselves to the accompaniment of the organ processional.

With each step she took, Andrea endeavored to keep her gaze on the stained-glass window at the front of the church. But she couldn't forget that Lucas Hastings was in the congregation and his presence distracted her. Everything somehow felt unreal as she finished her walk to the front and turned around.

Normally the hour-and-fifteen-minute service was the time when Andrea worshiped in the fullest sense of the word. But right now she was lost in a tumult of emotions. Helpless to do otherwise, she found her attention returning again and again to the man seated halfway back in the nave. The man whose handsome face and well-cut tan suit made him stand out from the other male worshipers.

There had been a time directly after the trial when she'd fantasized about Lucas Hastings, about meeting him under other circumstances and getting to know him better. But that was before she'd experienced firsthand the dark side of his unpredictable nature. Once more, shame consumed her as she recalled the way she'd flung her arms around his neck and sought his lips in an action designed only to protect him, never dreaming that their mouths would fuse in passion or that his kiss would blot out the rest of the world.

So deep was her turmoil, that Paul's inspired sermon about detours and new beginnings barely registered on her consciousness. When it dawned on her how far her mind had wandered, she chastised herself severely and made a concentrated effort to listen.

What she heard led her to surmise that if any parishioners had come to the service harboring negative feelings about others, Paul's words would have made them look inwardly at their own faults and do a little repenting.

Without a doubt, the issue of Lucas Hastings's worthiness to function in society had prompted Paul to choose his particular topic. Andrea couldn't help but admire the senior pastor who, in front of an entire congregation, including the censorious Margo Sloan, boldly championed a known sinner.

But not a confessed one, an inner voice nagged. And it seemed that just then her glance met Lucas Hastings's across the expanse. For a moment she was transported back to the courtroom, back to those few seconds when his eyes had revealed raw pain and confusion before he was handcuffed and taken away.

Even though he had paid the penalty and was ready to resume his rightful place in society, the question of his guilt or innocence loomed larger in her mind than ever.

Why? What does it matter? For what possible reason could anything to do with Lucas Hastings be of concern to her now?

Afraid of the answer, she escaped through a side door at the conclusion of the service and went directly to her office. A steady stream of people needing to talk about confirmations, blessings and marriages kept her so busy she didn't have time to worry about the evening ahead. At least, not until she got into her car to drive home.

Then the thought of what might happen if she let Lucas Hastings into her apartment descended on her in full force, and before she knew it she had run a stop sign, missing a car coming the other way by mere inches. The driver was angry, and rightfully so. He blasted his horn for long seconds while she drove on, shaking.

But she didn't know if the reaction was due to her near accident or to Lucas Hastings's unexpected reappearance in her life—at the precise moment she had begun to think she'd put the whole affair behind her.

CHAPTER FOUR

ANDREA SURVEYED the nine people assembled in her living room. So far Barbara and her mother hadn't arrived. Nor had Lucas Hastings.

Knowing how much he enjoyed shocking her, Andrea supposed he might have threatened to come to the house without ever intending to follow through. His idea of retribution had caught her off guard in ways she never would have imagined. A man who had spent time in prison was capable of almost anything, she supposed, and she bitterly resented his intrusion in her life.

The irony was that she had no one to blame but herself. She had created the situation. All afternoon her adrenaline had been working overtime as she contemplated his arrival and the disastrous evening ahead. Every time the doorbell rang, her body broke out in fresh perspiration.

She checked her watch again. "It's ten after seven," she said to the group. "Even though I'm expecting some other people, I think we'll start the video so that we'll have time for discussion afterward. It's called *Coping in Crisis*. I obtained it through a psychology professor at the seminary in Oakland. I've never seen a better treatment of this subject. The whole parish ought to view it."

Everyone responded with enthusiasm and agreed they shouldn't wait any longer.

"Let me help," Ned Stevens offered with a wide smile, quickly switching off the lights as Andrea turned on the VCR. He was one of the men Doris had insisted was more than a little interested in Andrea. It wasn't the first meeting he'd attended, and his early arrival, as well as his eagerness to help her set up the folding chairs she'd borrowed from the church, led Andrea to believe Doris was right.

Upon obtaining a divorce from the wife who had deserted him, the sandy-haired pharmacist had moved into the parish with his two young children, toddlers he was raising on his own. Andrea felt real compassion for him and, except for Mark, she'd never met a nicer person. But a relationship with him, other than pastor and parishioner, wasn't possible, not only because of the rules concerning lay members and clergy, but because she felt no attraction, no fire.

As soon as she sat down on the couch, the bell rang. Nervously she got to her feet and started for the door, but Ned beat her to it. When it was Mabel rather than Lucas Hastings who hurried inside and took the seat Andrea had just vacated, Andrea had a hysterical urge to scream, and she sagged against the nearest wall for support.

Mabel had never come to the Sunday-night sessions before. Which meant that Margo Sloan had been busy on the phone. Thankful for the darkness, Andrea buried her face in her hands, wondering how she would cope with an increasingly complicated situation.

Though the documentary offered solutions for dealing with most crises, it presented no guidelines for handling an unknown quantity like Lucas Hastings. Andrea was seriously considering calling off the rest of the evening's activity and asking everyone to go home. She'd follow them out the door and drive over to Doris's to spend the night.

"Your phone is ringing." Several of the group spoke at once. Embarrassed because she'd been so preoccupied with mutinous thoughts, she mumbled her thanks and hurried into the kitchen to answer it. Since her budget allowed only one phone, she'd had it installed in the kitchen where she could talk to people and take notes at the breakfast table if necessary.

Afraid she might hear Lucas Hastings's voice on the other end, she hesitated before picking up the receiver. But it turned out to be Barbara, who said her mother was too tired to attend the meeting. Andrea assured her she understood, told her she'd drop by later in the week and thanked her for calling.

The momentary reprieve lulled her into a false sense of security. She pushed open the door connecting the kitchen to the living room, feeling confident that because the meeting had been under way for some time, Lucas Hastings wouldn't be making an appearance, after all. But she was mistaken. Out of nowhere strong hands grasped her around the waist, bringing her to a full stop. "Sorry to be late," he whispered in the semidarkness. Whether on purpose or not, his lips grazed the softness of her hot cheek. "I slipped in while you were on the phone."

Several heads, including Ned's and Mabel's, turned in their direction. Andrea swallowed hard, unable to believe any man could be so outrageous. Yet her body was already responding to his touch, and she hated the excitement he could engender with even the slightest contact.

"You've never been sorry for anything in your life!" she muttered furiously, as angry with herself as with him. Not caring what anyone else would think, she jerked away from him. He surprised her by letting her go without a struggle. And though there were several empty chairs among the group assembled around the television set, he chose the seat next to Ned's, which Andrea suspected the other man had been saving for her.

Ned's frown confirmed her suspicions. And the satisfied curl of Lucas Hastings's arrogant mouth told her he was perfectly aware of what he'd done. Once more Andrea leaned against the wall, this time suppressing her rage. She realized Lucas Hastings was a law unto himself and would stop at nothing to get what he wanted.

Again, she was confounded at her lack of insight into his true character. What had prompted her to protect him from the guard at the prison? How could she have done anything so *reckless?*

As soon as the video came to an end, Ned stood up and turned on the lights, but his usual warm smile was missing. He, along with the others, couldn't have missed what must have looked like an intimate exchange between her and Lucas Hastings. Their natural curiosity would lead them to draw erroneous conclusions, and word would spread throughout the entire parish in a matter of days.

Andrea would have given anything to simply vanish from the room. Looking for a way out, she motioned to Deanna Miles to help her with the refreshments. The divorced mother, whose son had been crippled in a tragic bike accident a few years earlier, willingly followed Andrea to the kitchen.

When they'd cut the homemade brownies into squares and put them on plates with a scoop of ice cream, she asked Deanna to do the serving. When she no longer had any excuse to stay in the kitchen, Andrea went back to the living room carrying a tray of glasses filled with ice water, which she put on the coffee table so people could help themselves. Taking one for herself, she found a chair as far away as possible from Lucas Hastings. She joined in the conversation going on around her but refused to acknowledge his presence.

As soon as she was seated, however, Melanie Hall, the spokesperson for the group, said, "We've been waiting for you, Pastor. Luke here is the shy type, and he'd like you to make the official introduction, since he says you're the inspiration for getting him out to church in the first place."

Andrea choked on her drink. The icy water spilled onto the rose velveteen chair Mabel had lent her. Shy! What a joke! she cried helplessly to herself, scrubbing the water spots with a paper napkin. She didn't dare look at him for fear she might lose her temper in front of her parishioners.

"I think maybe the Pastor's afraid of offending my sensibilities." His words filled the awkward moment of silence. Forgetting to keep up her guard, she lifted her head, but he was turned away from her and she couldn't read his expression. "The fact is, I've spent the last six months at the federal prison in Red Bluff for the crime of fraud."

His blunt declaration had everyone's attention now, including Andrea's. She waited expectantly for him to tell the others that he wasn't guilty of the crime. But the words didn't come.

Part of her admired him for stating the plain awful truth without attempting to justify himself. Another part of her folded in on itself like the petals of a flower no longer warmed by the sun. Perhaps Lucas Hastings was finally admitting the truth—that he had broken the law.

"But you've paid your dues and that's all behind you, right?" Arnold Lems said. Arnold had been forced to declare bankruptcy a few years earlier. He'd found a new job and was endeavoring to pay back his creditors, but it was a slow, painful process.

Lucas Hastings sat forward in the folding chair, his hands clasped between his legs. "I'll never be able to forget the experience, but yes, I've done my time and I'd like to get on with my life."

He sounded perfectly serious now, and Andrea found herself listening to the rich cadence of his voice as if her very existence depended on it. "There's a scripture I recall from childhood. It goes something like, 'When I was in prison, ye visited me.'" Several in the group nodded. "I'd forgotten about it until Pastor Meyers came to Red Bluff."

Drawn against her will, Andrea looked incredulously at him, and for a moment it felt as though they were the only two people in the room.

"After her sermon, I made arrangements with the guard to talk to her, but I'm afraid I let the conversation get out of hand and I said some pretty unforgivable things. In fact, my behavior left so much to be desired that I could have been in serious trouble with the guard, enough to be moved to another prison with tighter security. But the pastor here came to my rescue." He leveled his gaze on her. "I'll never forget that she comforted me in my darkest hour."

A white-hot heat consumed Andrea's body as she remembered the very intimate and personal nature of her comforting.

"Would it surprise you to know that no one in my life has ever been that brave or done anything that unselfish for me?"

Tears threatened behind Andrea's eyelids, and judging by the total quiet in the room, the others had been equally moved by his comments. He'd sounded so sincere Andrea didn't know what to believe.

"It doesn't surprise me," Arnold muttered in a choked-up voice. "Not one bit. Andy's got a heart of gold."

Melanie let out a compassionate sigh that seemed to reflect the sentiments of the group, with the possible exception of Mabel, who always managed to look so cross it was hard to tell what she was thinking. "Luke, we're all aware of your background. What are your plans for the future?"

Andrea hated to admit to anyone, let alone herself, that she wanted answers to that very question—and a good many more.

"Most people don't realize that once you've been convicted of this type of crime, the Securities Exchange Commission bars you from the stock exchange for five years."

"Then you're unemployed right now?" Deanna asked anxiously.

"That's right."

Mabel sat primly in her chair. "I would imagine it's difficult to get work when people know you've been in prison."

Andrea cringed at Mabel's lack of tact, and worse, at her lack of sensitivity toward another human being.

Luke eyed the older woman shrewdly. "I don't know the answer to that yet, but I have a few options I'm looking into."

"The grocery store in my neighborhood has been advertising for a cashier," Radie Ormsby, a member with Lou Gehrig's disease, interjected. "I realize it would be a far cry from what you've been doing, but if you're short of cash, it could help you out. If you're interested, I'll put in a good word for you." Her suggestion started a deluge and soon everyone, even Ned, had an idea about where he might find work. What they didn't know, Andrea thought privately, was that with or without a job, Lucas Hastings had financial resources to fall back on.

"I appreciate all your suggestions," he said in a sincere voice, his steady gaze encompassing everyone in the room. "And if none of my plans materialize, I'll take you up on them."

"Pastor Meyers has helped several people in our congregation get positions," Arnold offered. "She was the one who told me about the job I'm in now and vouched for me."

Luke raised his head and looked at Andrea. After the way he'd held his audience spellbound, she wasn't in the least surprised at their warm reception. "She and Pastor Yates have already done more than enough. Perhaps some of you don't know I've been put to work coaching the volleyball team."

Mabel regarded him as if he were an alien. "Do you have the proper qualifications?"

"Aside from the fact that I played the game every day in prison, I was captain of the championship varsity volleyball and baseball teams during my undergraduate days at Princeton."

With that startling revelation, Mabel was well and truly put in her place. Andrea jumped up and began gathering glasses and dishes to take to the kitchen. She needed a few minutes alone to sort everything out in her mind. She sensed that until tonight she'd only seen a little of the real Lucas Hastings—like the tip of an iceberg visible above the water. But now she'd been allowed a glimpse of the mysterious depths beneath the surface and she had to admit she was fascinated, in spite of her misgivings.

Ned followed her into the kitchen. "The others are getting ready to leave, but I'd like to stay and help clean up. Do you mind?"

She'd half expected something like this. She was on the verge of telling Ned that a personal relationship was out of the question when she discovered Luke only two steps behind him, carrying more glasses and napkins.

"Actually, I have an appointment with the Pastor right now," Luke said with a pleasant smile. "I made it at church this morning—through Doris."

Andrea was appalled at his audacity. Surely he couldn't be the same man who moments ago had almost convinced her of his compassion and vulnerability!

Ned's face wore a decided scowl. "Another time, then," he muttered, and left the kitchen. She swept past Luke, ignoring his condescending smile, as she hurried out to placate Ned. But the minute she entered the living room, everyone converged to thank her for the evening, and by the time all the good-nights were said, Ned was nowhere to be found.

"Alone at last," Luke murmured from behind her. "I thought they'd never leave."

Andrea whirled around in panic. Her movements were nervous and awkward as she started straightening the furniture. He was too close, too unpredictable, too appealing. Dressed in a lightweight suit of smoky blue and a paisley tie, he looked as though his energy and sophistication had not been affected in any way by six months in prison. And worse, his physical presence was so sensually disturbing she had a hard time remembering who he was and what he'd done.

"That was a very unkind remark, considering how you just won their sympathy with a few well-chosen words."

"The truth doesn't usually take more than that," he said matter-of-factly, throwing her into confusion again. "But before you say another word, let's get one thing clear. I found the members of your flock to be honest, caring, decent people and I look forward to getting to know each of them better. But not tonight."

Andrea grabbed one of the folding chairs, clutching it with tense fingers, and carried it to the walk-in hall closet she used for storage. He anticipated her movements and opened the door. As soon as she put it against the wall, she knew she'd made a mistake. He was blocking the doorway when she turned to leave.

"You have no idea how much I've been waiting for this moment."

All the teasing was gone from his voice. Andrea's pulses started to race, because she knew exactly what he was talking about. Kissing him again had been on her mind, too—from the moment she'd seen him last week.

"I-it's gratifying to know you've undergone a spiritual conversion during your confinement, Mr. Hastings."

His devilish smile heightened her nervous excitement. She was trapped in her own home by a man who had barely been released from prison. A man who had wrung a physical response from her that had changed her perception of herself. He'd made her realize she was a flesh-and-blood woman with needs and desires. He'd made her hunger for things she had dismissed, passions she'd thought unnecessary. And somehow, with that extraordinary sixth sense of his, he knew it. . . .

"The last time we were alone together I distinctly heard you call me Luke, *darling*."

She could hardly swallow. "We both know why I did that."

"Admit your gesture wasn't just in the name of altruism."

"I admit no such thing."

"Why? Because you're embarrassed to admit you're as attracted to me as I am to you? Is that because of your work—or because of my past? Or maybe a little of both?"

She backed farther into the closet.

"Why didn't you come back to the prison? Was it because you were afraid the same thing might happen again?"

Through clenched teeth she said, "The prison service is Paul's domain."

"As it should be. A men's penal institution is no place for a woman like you. Much as I wanted to see you again, I hoped I'd scared the living daylights out of you so you wouldn't come back."

"You're managing to do that right now without even touching me."

His eyes narrowed on her mouth. "That was my biggest mistake. Touching you."

Nervously she slid her hands into the pockets of her jacket. "I can't see that anything's being accomplished by this conversation."

"I disagree," he whispered. "During that trial I watched you and you watched me, though you're shaking your head in denial. Day after day we got to know each other a little better."

"That's absurd!"

But he kept on talking. "I realized from the start that I'd been framed and would probably lose the case, so I found myself fantasizing about you. About what it would be like to talk to you, to hold you, touch you. But nothing prepared me for what happened when my black-haired angel magically appeared at the prison and welcomed me into her arms with a kiss a man would die for."

Andrea gasped at his words. Could he read her mind? He had just described her own feelings, her own reaction. But she didn't dare admit that. "I think prison has distorted your perception of what went on," she said instead.

"On the contrary, it clarified many things for me."

"If you insist on talking about this, do you mind if we do it in the living room rather than the closet? I...I suffer from claustrophobia."

"If that's true, you would never have entered a prison where a gate locks behind you at every turn."

His mind worked faster than she could think. "What do you want, Mr. Hastings?"

"Luke. And you know exactly what I want."

"Surely there must be a woman in your life...."

His mouth quirked. "There have been several, but none who've left a lasting impression. Certainly none who would have done what you did."

She supposed his comment could be taken in a variety of ways, and she didn't care to explore any of them. "What about that grief-stricken woman at your trial?" she asked before she could stop herself.

The expression on his face hardened. "She happens to be the wife of a good friend of mine who was killed in a plane crash a few years ago. Any feelings I have for her are strictly those of friendship. They certainly bear no resemblance to my emotions where you're concerned."

Andrea swallowed painfully. "I'm afraid all I did was manage to make a perfect fool of myself and intrude on your privacy."

"You mean my private hell," he amended. "You're an enigma, Pastor. You voted against me at the trial, then came to my rescue at the prison."

She stared down at the floor to avoid looking at him. "If you'd gotten into trouble with the guard, I felt that indirectly it would have been my fault and I didn't want that to happen. Y-you'd suffered enough."

"Tell me something," he said softly. "Were you the juror who held up the proceedings? You were out long enough to make me wonder if there was hope, after all."

"I'm afraid that's privileged information," she said evasively.

His eyes blazed with emotion. "It *was* you. I knew it."

Andrea found she couldn't deny it. "I felt the evidence against you was too overwhelming, too one-sided. I couldn't imagine a man with your intelligence and knowledge of the stock market leaving a trail of mistakes even a child could follow. But in the end, the damaging evidence left me no choice except to cast a guilty vote."

After an interminable silence he said, "Thank you for your honesty."

Her face aflame, she added, "However, your behavior at the prison gave me some serious doubts about your innocence. And the longer you keep me in this closet, the more I'm convinced the jury reached the right verdict."

His low chuckle excited her, heightening her awareness of his sexual appeal. "Since that's the way you feel about me, it won't matter if I take what I want. What's one more black mark on my file?''

"Stay away from me, Mr. Hastings.'' It was frightening to feel this kind of response to a man, to feel so out of control around him. She feared he could make her do whatever he wanted without even trying.

"Ask me anything but that.''

"Mr. Hastings, I'm a pastor!''

"You're a woman who happens to be a pastor, and right now you're not wearing your collar. The fact that you didn't put it on although I warned you I was coming makes me wonder if you've been waiting for me just as eagerly.''

Could he be right? Has she subconsciously left it off for that reason? She dismissed the thought abruptly and decided to switch tactics. "If I give you what you want, will you go away and promise to leave me alone from now on?''

"How could I possibly promise that when we'll be seeing each other tomorrow and every weekday afternoon for volleyball practice until the tournament?''

"I could change your status as coach with one phone call to Paul.''

"Do that and you're certain to disappoint the kids, as well as lose any chance at the championship. But you won't be getting rid of me, because I intend to become a fully involved member of the parish. We'll be seeing each other at choir practice, study groups, Sunday worship services. The list is endless.''

Andrea was totally baffled. "Why? You don't even believe in God.''

"I believe in you. Whether you like it or not, you've held my salvation in your hands for quite some time now."

"Your *salvation?*"

"I've already explained that your visit to Red Bluff came at my darkest hour. It's not something I'm likely to forget." His voice was quiet, and Andrea was more terrified than ever—not of him but of her own intense response.

"If you touch me, I'll scream, and Mabel downstairs will hear me and call the police," she threatened. "Y-you'll be back in prison before the night's over!"

"I'll risk it."

As he started for her, Andrea backed farther into the closet, pressing against the clothes that hung there. "Stop this right now, Luke." Her breathing had grown shallow, her voice hoarse and croaking. "We're adults, for heaven's sake."

"Mmm," he murmured, coming closer until his arms went around her and he gathered her against him. "Consenting adults. That's what makes it so perfect. I'm going to kiss you, Andrea Meyers, and if you want to prove to me that God's in his heaven, you'll kiss me back. You'll kiss me because you *want* to. Because you can't help yourself."

"You're going to regr—" But the rest of her threat turned into a mindless moan as his mouth closed over hers. It was exactly like before. Only this time there were no observers, no one to tell Lucas Hastings to get back to his cell. There was nothing and no one to prevent Andrea from being swept out to sea by the riptide, and she found herself kissing him back with abandon.

"I'm beginning to believe someone heard my prayers, after all," Luke whispered huskily as his lips roved over her face, leaving a trail of moist kisses from her eyelids to her chin.

Their bodies were so perfectly attuned Andrea experienced actual physical pain as she summoned every vestige of willpower to separate herself from him. She was way out of her depth, drowning in the emotions he roused in her.

"I'm not ready to let you go," he groaned as she pulled free and escaped to the living room, trying to regain her equilibrium.

With her back toward him she said in a firm, controlled voice, "Now that you've gotten that out of your system, please go and leave me alone."

"If you think that was enough to satisfy me, then you don't know much about men."

"Nor you about women." She turned to him, her hands balled into fists at her sides. "Indulging yourself with the first available female after six months' deprivation isn't—" She broke off, maddened by his taunting smile.

"I agree things got pretty exciting in that closet, if not a little out of hand. But let's be honest, Andrea. What we were doing was kissing each other. I wasn't exactly forcing myself on you—was I? You were part of it."

He closed the distance between them and planted a hard kiss on her mouth, as if he had every right to touch her whenever and wherever he wanted. "When

I decide to *indulge* myself, you'll know all about it. Because you'll be there with me.''

"Your fantasies are going to get you into serious trouble," she warned icily.

"I'm already there. And you're the reason." His voice was low, dangerously soft. "Just remember, you were the one who dared to enter the devil's territory. It's on your head, Pastor. I know you're as frustrated as I am, so I'm not going to wish you good-night. Sleep will be a long time in coming—for both of us.''

CHAPTER FIVE

ANDREA LEFT HER OFFICE late the following Friday afternoon, carrying a gaily wrapped package.

Doris, who was leaving too, caught up with her. "You're not going to the hospital again? That makes five nights this week!"

"Mary Driscoll had a baby girl this morning. If I don't go over there now, I won't have time tomorrow because of the youth outing."

"Let Paul take the kids bowling. You need a day off!" Doris exclaimed.

"I can't right now." In truth, Andrea didn't want time to herself in case Luke decided to come by the apartment when he thought she'd be home. After what had happened on Sunday night, she vowed never to find herself alone with him again. As a result, she'd crammed two weeks' worth of activities into one, which gave her the excuse she needed.

Because she had to be a part of the volleyball team, she couldn't avoid seeing him altogether. But each day she made a point of leaving practice ten to fifteen minutes before the others. That way Luke couldn't detain her and she avoided any personal conversation—or worse.

As time went on, however, her worries that he might do something to embarrass her in front of the parish teenagers proved groundless. Whatever he said or did when the two of them were alone, his behavior on the court couldn't be faulted. His athletic expertise was obvious. The kids were in awe of him. So was Andrea. She did everything in her power not to let it show, but it was hard, if not impossible, to remain indifferent.

Luke was endowed with many gifts; he was also fiercely competitive, an attitude that infected everyone on the team. He had them convinced that if they came faithfully to practice, followed his game plan and kept themselves in shape, they'd have a good chance of winning the all-church trophy.

By the time Saturday arrived, Andrea was beginning to believe that she had nothing more to fear from Luke. He hadn't once stepped out of line or referred to what had gone on between them. He'd made no obvious attempt to see her and hadn't left even one message with Doris—something she'd suspected he might do. She had no idea how he filled his hours or what he did when he wasn't coaching ball, and she told herself she didn't *want* to know.

That was a lie, of course. She was consumed with curiosity about every detail of his life. Particularly when it came to women.... No man as attractive and virile as Lucas Hastings lacked beautiful women in his life. For all she knew, he was with a different one every night of the week.

Andrea didn't kid herself for a second that he meant what he'd said about becoming an active member of the congregation. After the way she'd thrown herself at him in the prison, he'd done what any red-blooded man would do—taken advantage of the situation. Paul had suggested as much.

But his ardor seemed to have cooled, and even though she'd initially distrusted his motives in coming to the church looking for volunteer work, she could see that the coaching job brought him pleasure and helped fill his free time while he was at loose ends. Once the tournament was over, he'd probably move on to a new challenge, and her life would settle down to the way it was before.

The trouble was, she could no longer imagine her world without Lucas Hastings in it. Somehow he'd managed to get under her skin during the trial, and he was still there, penetrating a little deeper every day, taking over her thoughts and feelings. If she wasn't careful, if she didn't guard her emotions zealously, he just might work his way into her heart.

When she pulled into the church parking lot the next morning, a bitterly cold Saturday, Richie, Dwayne, Casey and Matt separated themselves from the teenagers huddled on the steps and hurried over to Andrea's car, intending to ride with her.

She loved them all but had a special fondness for Matt, who'd been dealing with an alcoholic mother since childhood. Andrea had made herself available to him whenever he needed to talk. On occasion, when he couldn't handle being at home, she'd let him sleep on her couch. They'd become the best of friends.

He opened the front door on the passenger side and got in. The others climbed in the back.

"We thought maybe you weren't coming."

She gave Matt a mock frown. "Have I ever let you down?"

"I don't know. I'll have to think about it."

Andrea nudged him playfully. "Who's driving the rest of the kids?"

"Well, the Millers have already taken one group and Pastor Yates is taking the rest. He's locking up the church right now. Let's go. We're going to be late."

She rolled her eyes. "I thought you guys weren't all that excited about going bowling. I seem to remember several complaints at practice yesterday."

"Yeah," Casey said. "When Luke found out how we felt, he talked Pastor Yates into taking us flying instead."

"Flying?"

Matt eyed her skeptically. "Didn't you know he's a pilot?"

"Lucas Hastings is a *pilot?*"

"Yeah," they said in unison. "He has his own plane and he's going to give each of us a ride over the city," Richie explained.

"But at this rate, by the time we get to the airport, everybody else will be ahead of us," Matt muttered.

Andrea blinked in astonishment before saying, "Just a minute. I'll be right back."

While the boys groaned, she jumped out of the car and ran over to Paul, who was herding the rest of the kids into his car. He smiled when he saw her. "We couldn't have asked for a more perfect day to go flying, could we?"

She had to admit that despite the low temperatures the cloudless blue sky was all they could have hoped for. "No," she muttered, but her thoughts weren't on the weather. "Paul, I had no idea the plans had been changed."

"I tried to reach you several times last evening and again this morning, but you were out. As you know, the kids weren't that excited about going bowling in the first place. The minute Luke mentioned he'd take them flying, they got hold of parents for permission and the plans were all set.

"Andy," he murmured when she didn't say anything, "the man's been flying since he was sixteen years old. Don't let his prison record warp your common sense. Do you really think he'd put the children's lives at risk?"

"No, of course not." She shook her head. "It's not that. I suppose I'm surprised he's getting so involved with our youth group." *Just as he threatened.* If she didn't have to drive the boys, she'd back out right now because she was afraid—afraid that the more time she spent with Luke, the more necessary he would become to her life.

"I think it's a wonderful gesture on his part. He has a natural rapport with the the kids. I can already see the bonding that's taking place. We've needed someone like him for a long time. If things continue at this rate, I wouldn't be surprised if the council recommends him to be a youth leader."

But he wasn't a member of the parish, and Andrea couldn't imagine parish life holding his interest for long. She felt strangely bereft at the thought.

Paul's words haunted her all the way to the small airport outside Albuquerque. For once she didn't pay much attention to the boys. Luke had given Richie instructions on how to find the hangar, and Andrea located it with little difficulty.

When they soon joined the others they learned that Luke was flying with Lisa. One of the others had already been up in the plane and couldn't stop rhapsodizing about the fact that Luke had let him handle the controls for part of the flight.

As the teenagers waited impatiently for their turns, Andrea counted heads, noting in dismay that Betsy Sloan wasn't among them. Had Margo kept her from coming? But she didn't have time to dwell on the situation, because the blue-and-white twin-engine Beechcraft approached for its landing. When it taxied to a stop in front of the hangar, Andrea's eyes fastened on Luke, seated in the cockpit. Except for his hair, she wouldn't have recognized him in his sunglasses and headset. If he saw her standing with the others, he gave no indication.

One by one, the kids climbed into the plane for their ride. By the time Paul's turn came around, most of the group had made up their minds to take flying lessons. If Luke had wanted to win them over, he'd picked the perfect activity. The poor parish would never be the same. *And neither would she!*

Paul was grinning from ear to ear as he emerged from the plane and called to Andrea, "You're next!"

Her heart started to race and she felt her stomach lurch in excitement and fear. "I don't think so. I've never flown in anything but a 727."

"Chicken!" the kids taunted.

Paul winked at her. "If this old man enjoyed it, I can promise you it's an experience you shouldn't miss."

The longer she stood there making an issue of it, the more ammunition she provided Luke, who knew exactly why she was hesitating. The last thing she wanted was to let him know how much power he had over her, how strongly she was drawn to him, body and soul. It seemed that every time they were together, another dimension of his fascinating personality manifested itself, enchanting her a little more. In light of what she was learning about him, she was increasingly convinced that he *couldn't* have cheated his own clients.

"Go on," Matt urged. "It's fantastic."

"Say a prayer for me," she shouted over her shoulder. She walked toward the plane, feeling light-headed and a bit queasy.

The warm interior felt comforting after the hours she'd spent standing outside in the cold. Luke flashed her a brilliant smile as she took her place in the co-pilot's seat and fastened the belt. "Welcome aboard."

The tone of his voice said he'd been waiting for her and knew she'd finally come to him of her own accord.

"I might as well tell you right now I've never been up in a light plane before," she murmured, trying to disguise her sudden elation.

"The sensation's addictive—and not all that different from the way we feel whenever we get into each other's arms."

Her face grew hot and she refrained from looking at him. "You have a one-track mind."

"It runs right alongside yours." His seductive chuckle electrified her. Desperate to change the subject, she started to speak, but by that time he was talking to the control tower, making further conversation impossible.

The next thing she knew, they were taxiing out to the runway. Airport traffic was heavy, and they had to wait for several planes before it was their turn. After takeoff she felt as though her stomach lay somewhere on the ground. But when they reached cruising altitude, she'd recovered sufficiently to look out the window at the spectacular view. All the while, though, her thoughts were on the man beside her.

How could he have stood being locked up for six months after experiencing this kind of freedom?

"Thinking about times like this helped me keep my sanity while I was in jail," he said.

"It must have been a dreadful experience," she said, awed by the way their thoughts were so closely and inexplicably linked. She kept her attention trained on the city below.

"Tell me something," he said quietly. She turned solemn eyes toward him. "How is it you could see through that masquerade of a trial when no one else did?"

His question sounded offhand, yet she knew he never said or did anything without a reason. She wished she could remove his dark glasses and peer into his eyes, because at odd unguarded moments they gave away secrets.

"I'm sure there were others in the courtroom besides me who felt the prosecution's case was too neatly stacked."

"You must be referring to my attorney," he said wryly. "But I'm talking about the jury."

She took a deep breath. "We were told to find you guilty beyond a reasonable doubt, and you must admit the evidence against you was pretty overwhelming."

"But because Pastor Andy has a soft heart, she wanted to believe in me anyway, is that it?" he asked in a mild voice.

"Naturally I hoped your attorney would be able to come up with something to baffle the prosecutor. The entire jury hoped for that. But there was nothing to use in your defense. It all reminded me of a hurtful experience in my own past, which made me doubt your guilt."

"What hurtful experience? You know every skeleton in my closet while I have yet to learn anything about Andrea Meyers, the woman."

She stared at the gauges without seeing them. "It happened a long time ago. It isn't important."

"In other words, you're not ready to talk about it yet. So tell me, have you always lived in Albuquerque?"

"No."

The protracted silence exaggerated the drone of the plane's engines. Andrea sat there uncomfortably, staring out the window. Luke finally spoke. "Is it because I'm an ex-convict that you don't feel you can confide in me?"

"Of course not!"

"I know you're not indifferent to me. So if what you just said is true, then I have to assume there's something painful in your past you haven't resolved. I know a lot about that kind of situation," he murmured.

Andrea didn't have a defense against his innate honesty, and there was no question the man had suffered in ways she didn't even want to think about. Almost without volition, she found herself opening up to him. "Aside from the last two years, I lived all my life in California."

"Does your family still live there?" he asked softly.

"I have no idea." Luke's puzzled expression prompted her to explain. "I know very little about my parents except that they were living in Oakland, California, when I was born. According to a social worker familiar with my case, my teenage mother was disowned when her parents found out she was pregnant with me. Her boyfriend ran off and she had to rely on a state agency to help her get through the pregnancy. After I was born she abandoned me because she couldn't handle the responsibility and had no financial support."

His head turned in her direction. "What about your adoptive parents?"

"I was never adopted. I lived with several sets of foster parents."

"That couldn't have been easy."

"Actually, most of them were very good to me. But when I was around sixteen, my foster father lost his job, and because of various financial difficulties I was sent to live with another set of foster parents."

"Go on," he urged when she didn't continue right away.

"I liked them well enough, but their divorced son started dropping by the house when they weren't there." Luke muttered an oath she couldn't quite decipher. "The first time he tried to touch me I got frightened, and did everything I could to stay away from him. But he kept coming around and finding ways to see me when I was alone, so I ran away."

"Then what happened?" She could tell he was restraining his anger.

"The police picked me up, and my social worker conducted an investigation. It turned into a horrible experience with no one believing me because the son lied and because the parents supported his story. They had a reputation as excellent foster parents."

"I think I can figure out the rest," Luke said in disgust.

"I was accused of being manipulative and trying to seduce their son, which was a blatant lie. From junior high on, I'd maintained an *A* average and got on the honor roll every term. Most of my spare time was spent studying or helping with housework. I couldn't possibly have done all the things they said I'd done.

"In hindsight, I can see that they were trying to protect their son. He'd probably done things like that before. But I was only sixteen and I didn't understand. It was a nightmare. I was labeled a liar. And although my social worker got me out of that household, I had the feeling she didn't really believe me, either."

"Thank God she had the presence of mind to do that much for you."

"Naturally I was relieved to be removed from the situation, but at that point I felt truly alone in the world. No one believed me or stood by me. Not a single soul." She paused to take a breath and turned to look at Luke.

"During your trial, as the prosecution kept presenting more evidence against you, pounding you down, I started remembering my own experience. All my actions were construed the wrong way, just like yours. I looked at your partners and began to wonder if they'd set things up to frame you, exactly the way I'd been framed. I suppose it's for those reasons I had doubts about your guilt. The problem was, there was no tangible evidence, nothing the jury—"

"Andrea," he interrupted in a low voice.

But she couldn't stop now. "I thought about you many times in the weeks that passed," she went on. "I even remembered you in my prayers. When I saw you at the prison, I understood why my presence there angered you so much. You must have thought me hypocritical to condemn you on the one hand, then preach to you on the other. But I'd like you to know that regardless of your guilt or innocence, I didn't want you to suffer any more. I didn't want you to feel the intense loneliness and isolation I once did."

In the silence that followed she felt his hand reach for hers. She watched in wonder as he drew it to his lips and pressed a fervent kiss against the palm. Heat spread to her fingers and built in degrees until it traveled to every cell of her body. She let out an involuntary gasp that brought Luke's head around. She pulled back her hand.

"I finally have the truth," he said with a strained sigh. "Are you up to one more question? What do you think about me now? Have you decided I'm guilty or innocent?"

She moistened her lips and moved restlessly in the seat. "Only you and God know the truth."

There was another pause. "If I told you I was guilty of the crime, would it make a difference?"

His question brought new pain, a pain that practically paralyzed her in its implications. *Was he trying to tell her that her instincts had been wrong?* She turned her head away.

"I asked you a question," he prodded with an intensity she'd never heard before.

"We're out of the courtroom now, Luke, and you've paid your debt to society. I'm not your judge and never wanted to be. That part is over."

He shook his head. "You know very well I'm talking about something entirely different, something personal—between us. Between you and me and nobody else."

"I...I'm afraid I don't know what you mean," she hedged, playing for time while she struggled to understand him. Was he intimating he wanted a relationship with her as much as she wanted one with him? And if so, what kind of relationship and for how long? Because Andrea knew that if she became more seriously involved with him, she'd want to belong to him forever.

Luke exhaled sharply. "I'll give you until tonight to figure it out and come up with an answer."

Her heart started to pound. "I'm afraid that tonight I have plans to go out to dinner." She glanced at her watch. "Shouldn't we be getting back? Everyone's going to be upset that we've been up for so long."

"I would have taken you back whenever you asked me," he stated coolly. She smarted from the implication that it was her fault they'd stayed up so long. A protest formed on her lips, but she had to keep silent because he'd begun talking to the tower. "Hang on," he alerted her as they started their descent.

She gripped the seat and couldn't hold back an anxious exclamation as the ground rushed up to meet them. It didn't dawn on her until they touched down on the landing strip that the surroundings didn't look the same as before. Her head swerved toward Luke in alarm. "This isn't the airport!"

"Well, if it isn't, we're in big trouble."

"Luke! You know what I mean. Where are we?"

He didn't say anything until they'd come to a complete stop near an unfamiliar cluster of hangars and light aircraft. Though he turned to her, she couldn't see his eyes, still hidden by his sunglasses. "Santa Fe."

"What?"

He removed the headset and unfastened his seat belt. Her stomach quivered with sensation when his hands slid across to undo hers. The action brought their faces close together; she could smell the subtle aroma of his shaving lotion.

"When was the last time you were here?"

She felt unaccountably shy and couldn't look at him. "Never. I've meant to come before now, but something always prevented me."

"Then you're in for a treat. Even if it is winter." He stole a lush kiss from her parted mouth.

"Luke!" she cried, dizzy from the intimate gesture. "We can't stay here. What about the kids and Paul? Everyone's waiting for us."

He shook his head. "Paul already made arrangements with some of the parents to drive the kids home from the airport."

Her eyes widened in astonishment. "But I have a dinner to get ready for later on."

"Don't worry." The charm of his smile fell over her like mist. "You won't miss dinner. I have a wonderful little restaurant in mind."

She edged away from him in exasperation. This was probably one of the most exciting things that had ever happened to her and here she was in her parka, jeans and an old shirt, with her hair pulled back in a French braid. Hardly the attire for the kind of place a man with his money and taste would frequent. He was casually dressed himself, in a short, dark brown leather jacket, jeans and a wine-colored cotton sweater. But the clothes only emphasized his lean masculinity. In fact, he looked like the personification of every woman's fantasy—certainly hers!

Andrea took a deep breath. "I'm serious, Luke. The New Mexico Council of Churches is having their semiannual dinner this evening. Paul and I are expected to attend."

"Paul's going to make your excuses. When I told him my plans, he agreed it was time you had a day off. You've been working too hard, he said, and you never know when to quit."

"You kidnapped me!"

"Would you have come otherwise?"

"You know I wouldn't," she grumbled. "Saturday is one of our busiest days." But she might as well have saved her breath. He had already turned his back and disappeared out the door of the plane.

When she positioned herself by the doorway, he called up to her. "I've always operated on the premise of seize first, negotiate later. It's equally applicable when dealing with a difficult woman.'' He opened his arms. ''Jump down to me, Andrea.''

She wanted to. She wanted to very much. That was what frightened her. Instead, she said, ''I think I prefer getting out the normal way.'' Since that kiss, she didn't trust herself within phoning distance of him, let alone anything that could lead to more physical contact.

''You're probably as hungry and thirsty as I am,'' he said. ''There's a canteen right over there where we can grab a quick bite. Then we'll get a taxi and drive into town.'' The minute she reached the ground his arm went around her waist, and he maintained his possessive hold throughout the rest of the afternoon and evening.

The hours with Luke became a time of enchantment for Andrea as they strolled in and out of the shops and art galleries of the charming city that still retained all the flavor of its Spanish-Pueblo Indian architecture. Because of his interest in archaeology, which he told her his grandfather had nurtured, Luke was able to impart some fascinating information about the prehistoric Tiwa Indians whose pueblo had formed the first site of Santa Fe.

Luke indulged her fascination with the folk-art museum, but he finally had to insist they leave so there would be time to eat dinner before they returned to Albuquerque.

Mexican food took on a whole new meaning. The food was exciting and subtle, nothing like the Tex-Mex fast food she'd eaten before. Though in truth she was so besotted with her dinner partner, she could have eaten sawdust and enjoyed it.

Andrea found herself totally engrossed as he teased, argued, laughed and sent private messages with his eyes that told her he was counting the seconds until they could be completely alone. Tucked away in a tiny candlelit alcove, with a mariachi band to entertain them, she felt truly alive, far away from the cares and worries of her vocation. Eager to know everything about him, she urged him to talk about his family.

"There isn't a great deal to tell," he said unemotionally. "And it's not all that interesting. When I was a boy my parents and older brother died in a car accident. My grandfather, who was a widower, decided to live the rest of his life through me. He had a pilot's license himself and he encouraged my interest in flying—actually bought me a plane before I'd even turned twenty. As you can tell, I was spoiled and pampered. Eventually he sent me out East to school to learn all there is to know about the art of making money. At his death he owned an enviable amount of real estate in our fair city, enabling me to set up a stockbrokerage at an age when most men are just starting to climb the corporate ladder."

Not interesting? She wanted to ask him a thousand questions about all the things he hadn't said. But they had more to do with feelings than facts, and Luke Hastings was probably the most private person she'd ever met in her life. And the most intriguing. She wanted this night to go on forever. She planned to live it to the fullest, then store the memory in a secret corner of her heart to cherish forever.

When it was time to go back to the airport, she rebelled at the brutal interruption. For the first time she understood how devastated Cinderella must have felt when the clock struck twelve, forcing her to leave the prince before the enchantment wore off and she found herself a mere mortal once more.

Luke talked very little on the flight back. She assumed he needed all his concentration to fly at night. For her part, Andrea was too bemused by her attraction to him to say much of anything; she simply wanted to savor these last precious moments before the magic was gone.

The closer they flew to Albuquerque, however, the more remote Luke became. Every so often he turned an unsmiling face toward her. She couldn't imagine what was going through his mind, but it unnerved her so much that by the time they landed and climbed out of the plane, she'd already come back to earth with a vengeance.

Zipping her parka to the neck, she said stiffly, "Thank you for this day and evening. I think you can guess I've never had a more wonderful time in my life. But it's getting late and I must go. My car's right over there. You don't need to accompany me any farther."

"I've every need," he returned harshly. The same hand that had caressed hers until she'd wanted to climb over the dinner table and nestle in his lap now encircled her upper arm in an iron grip.

Her pulse raced triple-time as Luke ushered her past the hangar. She pulled the car keys from her pocket and unlocked the door. But the position of his body prevented her from getting in. She looked up at him in surprise.

"You've had more than enough time to figure out an answer. I'm still waiting."

Since Andrea knew better than to pretend she didn't understand what he was talking about, she said, "I have a lot to do before services in the morning. Could we discuss it next week after practice?"

"The question I asked only requires a yes or a no, not a lengthy dissertation."

She could have told him that after tonight she never wanted to be separated from him again. That if she let him, he could become her whole life and it didn't matter if he'd spent twenty years behind bars. But Luke was a man of sophistication and experience, and Andrea sensed that he was merely toying with her until he was ready to return to his own world, one totally removed from hers.

"Your silence speaks eloquently," came the caustic retort. "So, the pastor doesn't practice what she preaches."

"That's not it at all!" she cried, horrified that he'd read the wrong meaning. "I would have told Paul to get rid of you *last* Saturday if I couldn't see beyond your prison record."

He lifted her chin, the better to see her eyes, which he studied with soul-searching thoroughness. "Then why the hesitation?"

It took everything she possessed not to kiss the hand that cradled her face. "My life is the parish," she managed to say.

"I thought a stranger was welcome there."

"You are! For as long as you want to stay. Until you move on," she added quietly.

His fingers tightened on her chin. "Am I going someplace?"

"I don't know. Are you?" Her eyes implored him. "You have important decisions to make about the rest of your life—what kind of work will be meaningful to you now that you can't be a stockbroker. For one thing, you might have to relocate." That was what worried her most. That one day he'd leave.

"It's true my life is in transition right now."

At his words she shuddered in pain because it wasn't the answer she wanted, needed, to hear. How could it be? They had nothing in common. Apart from everything else, he didn't have any religious beliefs, while she was an ordained minister. A relationship other than marriage wasn't possible for her, and she had no idea if Luke was even interested in marrying. A man who'd stayed single this long might not be. And even if he did want to marry, would he want a wife who was a pastor, of all things? Any way she viewed it, there was no hope of a permanent relationship between them. To continue seeing him would result only in further pain.

"I really have to go," she said urgently.

The depths of his eyes read like a blank page. "Far be it from me to keep you from your duties."

His hand slid away so she could get into the car. She saw his retreating back through the rearview mirror and experienced a staggering sense of loss. *What's happening to me?*

CHAPTER SIX

ON FRIDAY AFTERNOON of the following week, Andrea reported for volleyball practice as she always did. But for the first time since he'd started coaching, Luke was late. She told herself she was glad.

Having to act normally around him, having to pretend that his indifference to her since their trip to Santa Fe didn't bother her, put Andrea under a heavy strain and tested her self-control. She didn't want to behave differently around the kids, but she knew her nerves were frayed. Her emotions were closer to the surface than usual.

Richie took charge, and they started their practice without Luke. But after another ten minutes, Casey, who didn't have a dad around and was crazy about Luke, said he was going to call him at work and find out what was keeping him.

"Work?" Andrea repeated as she opened her office so he could call.

The brawny seventeen-year-old nodded, punching in a number he obviously knew by heart. "Yeah. He got a job last week."

"Doing what?"

"Flying air cargo for some company. Isn't that great?"

She was saved from having to respond when she heard Casey asking someone on the other end if he could speak to Luke Hastings.

Andrea felt as though someone had just kicked her in the stomach. Why hadn't Luke said anything about it that night in Santa Fe? He didn't need the job, surely, not with his assets. Or did he? Maybe he'd lost everything except his car and plane when he had to make restitution. Maybe the flying job was temporary and not, in his opinion, worth mentioning.

Andrea sank down in her chair. The judge said Luke had paid back everything owing, so it had never occurred to her that he might be in financial trouble. He certainly wasn't the type of person to divulge his problems. When she thought about it, she realized she didn't even know where—or how—he lived. Compared to being a stockbroker, flying for a cargo company would bring a mere pittance. He was used to dealing in hundreds of thousands of dollars.

She was deep in thought when she heard Casey slam down the receiver. Something was wrong. "Casey?"

He frowned darkly. "Luke was due back from a run several hours ago, but ran into bad weather. They're waiting to hear from him."

Andrea didn't like the sound of that but had no intention of letting on to Casey that she was worried. "I'm sure delays like that happen every once in a while. Remember, he's an excellent pilot."

"He's the best!" Coming from Casey, it was a compliment of the highest order. Luke could have no idea how much of an impact he'd made on these teenagers in such a short time. They never even mentioned his past, which proved her theory that young people were naturally forgiving. Luke's heart would be warmed if he knew how much they cared about him.

"Let's get back to the gym. Maybe he'll show up before we're through." She didn't really believe that, but wanted to reassure Casey and the others.

The practice continued though everyone felt miserable; Lisa was so anxious she burst into tears. After the game Andrea took the kids to a convenience store around the corner from the church for doughnuts. She postponed going on her hospital rounds because she thought it was more important to lighten their mood.

But it was foolish of her to think she'd succeeded in getting their minds off Luke. The minute they spied the store, the kids ran to the phone booth and clustered around while Casey made another call. Andrea hovered in the background, aware that her heart was pumping far too fast. At the pained look on Casey's face when he got off the phone, she felt a chill that had nothing to do with the bleak wintry day.

"There's still no word of him," Casey said.

"In this case, I'd say no news is the best news," Andrea said brightly after a pause.

Matt looked at her as though she were crazy. "Why do you say that?"

"Because if there'd been an accident, it would probably have been discovered by now. They said something about bad weather. No doubt Luke is safe and waiting for it to clear. I'll tell you what. Let me copy down that number and a little later I'll call and try to find out more information. When I do, I'll get word to all of you. How does that sound?"

Everyone nodded, but it

"People ignore teenagers. B

you're a pastor, you'll be able

"You think so, huh?"

"Yeah," he said, giving her a

"Who wants a doughnut?"

Several of the kids took her up

majority decided to head on home. Before Casey left,

she took down Luke's work number and promised to

phone the volleyball players as soon as she had news.

Judging by the glum look on everyone's face, it was

going to be a long night.

As soon as they'd gone, she called the number and

was given the same information as Casey. Andrea

found out that he worked for Reynolds Air Freight,

which had an office at the main airport.

By the time she'd gotten back to the church, she'd

made up her mind to drive to the airport and find out

what was going on. It was one thing to pretend all was

well in front of the kids, but quite another to be alone

with her fears. The temperature would fall below zero

before morning, and the thought of Luke stranded

somewhere, perhaps injured . . .

Driving on the freeway, she gave herself the same

reassuring talk she'd given Casey and the others, but

it didn't help. Nothing would alleviate her anxiety un-

til she could see Luke standing in front of her wearing

that devil-may-care smile of his.

It was at that moment she realized she'd fallen

headlong in love with him.

After parking in the short-term lot, she dashed in-

side the main terminal and had to ask half-a-dozen

people before she learned that the freight room itself,

pilots assembled, was in another building
ther.

Twenty minutes later she found her destination. A
man in his twenties wearing the Reynolds insignia on
his uniform gave her a frankly admiring stare when she
ran up to the counter out of breath. She could hear
laughter and talking coming from a connecting room
behind him.

"What can I do for you?"

The elastic band holding her ponytail had broken,
and her black hair spilled around her shoulders in
disarray. She smoothed the annoying strands out of
her face as she rushed to explain. "I understand Lucas Hastings is one of your pilots, and I want to know
if you've heard from him yet. His plane was due in
hours ago."

He eyed her speculatively. "Are you a relative?"

Something serious must have happened or he
wouldn't be asking her that question. Andrea felt the
room tilt. "No. But I am a friend. Please, won't you
give me some information?" she pressed anxiously.

He tugged on his earlobe. "What did you say your
name was?"

"I'm Andrea Meyers. Pastor of the church where
Luke's been coaching the teenagers in volleyball.
When he didn't show up for practice this afternoon,
everyone was upset."

"You're a pastor?" He was clearly incredulous, and
his eyes wandered appreciatively over her body. Only
then did she realize that she was still dressed in her
practice jersey and jeans beneath her parka.

"Please," she urged, ridiculously close to tears and
ready to shake him for his lack of sensitivity. She was

ner last night and left too early this morning to grab any breakfast.''

Andrea's eyes closed involuntarily. *I could have lost him.* ''How did you get back to Albuquerque?''

''On a bus.''

''You're kidding. Couldn't someone have flown down for you?''

He shook his head. ''The wind was too strong. In any case, the phone lines were down in Magdalena.''

''It's a miracle you're alive!'' she cried. ''And your poor plane. . . .''

He laughed gently. ''Don't worry—I was flying one of the company planes. Insurance will cover the damages. My Beechcraft is for pleasure only.''

''Oh.'' She felt extremely foolish, but there was so much about him she didn't know. ''Does your boss appreciate the fact that you risk your life every time you go up in the air for him?''

''My boss?''

''Mr. Reynolds, or whoever it is who owns the company that hired you.''

He laughed again, a full-bodied laugh this time. It emphasized his beautiful white smile and his unquenchable delight in life—and brought a jolt of pleasure that was almost pain to every pulse point in her body.

''What's so funny? I can't see that any of this is a laughing matter.''

''If you'd been listening carefully to a rundown of my assets at the start of the trial, you might have remembered that Reynolds Air Freight is one of several companies I own.''

At that startling bit of news, she swallowed the rest of her drink in one fiery gulp. It was true: she hadn't been able to concentrate on much during the first hour or two of the trial. His attraction had been so powerful she'd had to force herself to pay close attention to the testimony.

"Casey distinctly said you were hired as a pilot last week."

"Let's just say I hired myself because flying is what I love to do most."

Andrea frowned. "I thought you lived and breathed the stock market."

His eyes grew hard. "I did. For too many years. But prison made me see a lot of things differently. I was away from the cut-and-thrust politics of Wall Street long enough to realize I never want to go back to it."

After being accused and sentenced to prison for embezzlement, he could hardly be blamed for feeling as he did. And after the ordeal he'd lived through since early morning, he needed sleep, and plenty of it, to erase the fatigue lines from his face.

He'd had his drink and had finished off every crumb. When she looked into his eyes again, the bitterness had fled and in its place was a mysterious glint. She decided it was time to go.

"What else does Your Highness require before retiring?" she asked lightly.

"I've had my loaf of bread, my jug of wine. Now I want 'thou.'" In an effortless movement, he caught her wrist, and with a tiny cry she landed in his lap. His arms went around her and he drew her up against his heart.

I'll only stay here for a moment, Andrea promised herself. Instinctively she hid her face in his neck, breathing in the scent of his freshly scrubbed skin, savoring the texture with her lips. "Thank God you're alive." Until she felt his hands go still, she hadn't realized she'd spoken the words aloud.

"Are you thankful enough to go to bed with me?" The explicit question jarred her back to reality in a hurry, but his arms became a vise when she tried to get off his lap. "Have you ever slept with a man?" Andrea should have been used to his direct way of speaking by now, but she wasn't. "Have you ever been in love?"

She finally lifted her head from his shoulder and met his questioning gaze. "Yes."

She noticed the sudden tightening of his jaw. "To which question?"

Andrea's fingers played absently with a tendril of brown hair on his neck. "I've never made love with a man, if that's what you're asking. I fell in love with Mark when I first started college. His mother was an invalid and needed a live-in housekeeper. Thankfully I was too old at eighteen to be forced into another foster home. Mark advertised for a housekeeper to take care of her when he couldn't. I accepted the job because it gave me food and shelter, and a chance to go to school at night to get my degree."

"You left out Mark as one of the incentives," he broke in coldly.

"Except for the fact that he was the kindest man I had ever met, I wasn't aware of him in a . . . romantic way. Not at first. I was too happy being on my own to think about anything else. It wasn't until his mother passed away that I came to consider him as anything more than a dear friend.''

''Why aren't you married to him, then?'' The terseness of his question surprised her.

''We were on the way to our wedding rehearsal when a semitrailer veered across the median. He was killed instantly, and I lay paralyzed in a hospital bed for almost a year.''

''Good Lord.''

''That was not my finest hour,'' she said shakily. ''I cursed God, and decided I must have been cursed myself, because happiness always seemed to elude me.''

''When you talk about being paralyzed, do you mean your legs?''

''My whole body, from the neck down.''

He let out an expletive and grasped her hand tightly. ''If that's true, then how do you come to be sitting on my lap now?''

''At first the specialists assumed it was a spinal injury. But test after test proved it was something else. The psychiatrist told me I had a death wish and that's why I couldn't move.''

After an interminable silence he said, ''What brought you back to life? Your faith in God? The church?''

Andrea smiled slightly. ''I suppose, ultimately, yes. You see, none of my foster parents ever attended a church, so the experience was alien to me. Then Mark invited me to go to his. And the only reason I went with him was because it made him happy. He and his mom were very devout.''

Andrea heard herself talking and marveled that she felt so comfortable, so right, sharing the details of her story with Luke. She would never have imagined this happening when she thought back to their encounter at the prison.

"While I was in the hospital, people from Mark's church started coming to visit me. Some of them I had met casually, but most of them were total strangers who had no reason to drop by. But they did. They not only entertained me but encouraged me. I was flooded with gifts and cards and plants.

"But it was the older teenagers who were probably the most instrumental in my recovery. Someone at the church had organized them to come every day after school, rain or shine. At first they sat around playing their music, telling awful jokes, making me laugh.

"One of the boys, named Rod, loved card games. Poker was his favorite, and he'd get his buddies to play penny-ante stuff right on top of my bed while I was lying there." She glanced at Luke, grinning. "That's when I figured out why they kept coming to the hospital. Whoever was in charge never knew what they were up to, and of course I didn't discourage the kids because I was having too much fun." She smiled at the memory.

"Anyway, when it came my turn, Rod would pick up my hand, show me my cards and I'd tell him what I wanted him to do. I was in bed a long time without moving. Because of that I had hours and hours to think, and I learned to count cards and figure out how each of the kids played, what made their minds work. I'm positive the competitive spirit in me was born during those poker sessions. It got so I could hardly wait for them to arrive so we could get on with the game. I lived for those moments.

"On a particular day, when it was my turn—" she paused to clear her throat "—as Rod reached over to pick up my cards, I stopped him with my hand because I wanted to do it myself. The rest, as they say, is history."

"You really had a miraculous recovery." His voice was low and hoarse.

She nodded. "Yes. And all because of the unselfishness of those teenagers. Curiously enough, I found myself wanting to attend church to find out what it was that made them so...generous. With their time and with themselves. After a while I decided to become part of them. As a result, I no longer wanted to pursue a business degree, and the idea of doing something meaningful to help others began to take hold. When the local pastor suggested I attend divinity school on a scholarship, everything fell into place."

Luke lifted a strand of her hair and toyed with it. "Destiny has played strange tricks on both of us. We would never have met if I hadn't been brought to trial," he murmured, sounding very faraway. Andrea felt his hand tighten in her hair.

"No," she whispered. "And if I hadn't been selected for jury duty...." When he let go of her hair and pressed the car keys into her hand, she didn't understand and stared at him with a puzzled expression.

"Tonight I meant to ask you to share my bed. But that would be stretching your pastoral duties beyond their limits, and the way I'm feeling right now, nothing less than making love to you all night long would satisfy me. So hurry back to your parish while I'm still in the mood to let you escape."

CHAPTER SEVEN

ANDREA WAS IN Herb Wilson's new apartment, putting towels and dishes away in the kitchen cupboards, when she heard voices coming from the front room. She checked her watch. It was a few minutes after eight, so maybe Paul and Herb had arrived. She left what she was doing and went to the other room, almost bumping into Casey and Matt, who were carrying in a large console TV. Their friendly voices greeted her as they set it down by the cable hookup.

"Who donated that?"

"I did."

Andrea whirled around in time to see Luke, who was dressed for volleyball practice in shorts and T-shirt like the rest of them, walk through the front door carrying a comfortable-looking reclining chair upholstered in dark leather. Their eyes met, but the glazed look of desire she'd seen in them last night was gone. Its absence left her chilled.

"Good morning, Pastor."

"Good morning," she answered quietly. His courteous greeting couldn't have made it clearer that he was backing off. Last night they'd reached an impasse. Luke knew her well enough to realize she wouldn't sleep with him unless they were married. So unless he got to the point of wanting to marry her, he'd probably leave her alone from here on.

It was no good telling herself she'd always known this day would come. Who'd have guessed the attraction between them would grow to such proportions that in five short weeks they couldn't trust themselves to be around each other without wanting to go to bed together? Lying to herself was a waste of energy. She was painfully in love with Lucas Hastings and wanted to be joined to him in every way.

"Herb won't believe it when he sees what you've brought. Because of his arthritis, he doesn't get out much and I suspect television provides a great distraction. How did you find a furniture store open this early in the morning?"

"I didn't." His voice carried from behind the set, where he was attaching the wires with the boys' help. "This is the TV from my study and it hasn't been turned on for the better part of a year. I decided it ought to go where it would get some use."

"That was very generous of you, Luke," she said sincerely.

"It was nothing of the kind. Since I have two other TVs sitting around the house, I'm hardly deprived. Generosity implies giving up something of yourself. Something important."

That remark left her with nothing more to say but a lot to think about as she went back to the kitchen to finish putting the silverware in drawers.

She wondered why Luke never let anyone compliment him, why he denigrated every unselfish act he performed. As she was trying to fit one of the drawers back on its runners, he called to her from the doorway. "Practice starts at nine, Pastor. Try to be on time for a change." His comment annoyed her so much she felt like throwing the whole drawer at him, silverware and all.

Herb Wilson and Paul, along with some ladies from the church, arrived minutes after Luke and the boys had left. When she'd finished in the kitchen, Andrea went out to greet them. She saw immediately why they were exclaiming with such delight. Luke's generosity hadn't stopped at the TV. Herb now had a striped velvet love seat and a French provincial coffee table, on top of which was a foot-high stack of magazines ranging from *Time* to *Field and Stream*. The older man stood in the center of the room and wept. Paul's eyes were suspiciously bright; as for Andrea, her heart was ready to burst.

Margo Sloan was among the women who'd brought groceries to stock his shelves and refrigerator. She walked past Andrea on her way to the kitchen and said out of earshot of the others, "How on earth did *you* come up with all this?"

"Many people donated," Andrea answered calmly. Then with great relish she added, "I believe Lucas Hastings provided the furnishings for the living room."

The woman's shocked expression made Andrea want to laugh.

"Which leaves one to wonder if he paid for any of it," Margo said nastily. "Has his probation officer heard about this?"

"I happen to know that every piece came out of his own home."

Margo Sloan's eyes glittered with accusation. "Yes, everyone in the parish has noticed how close the two of you have become. If I were you, I'd be careful of the company I keep. Very careful."

"Please don't threaten me, Mrs. Sloan. Otherwise I'm going to bring the matter up before the church council myself. Lucas Hastings has every right to get on with his life, and as long as he's doing his part for the parish, all of us will continue to make him welcome."

"We'll see," the older woman countered.

Angry enough to realize she was capable of physical violence, Andrea excused herself and sought out Paul. "I'm going back to the church for volleyball practice."

"How's it coming?"

"You wouldn't recognize us as the same team."

Paul rubbed his hands together in anticipation. "The tournament was the major topic of conversation at dinner the other night. I purposely kept quiet about Luke. Can't take the risk of someone else stealing our coach away from us."

"The kids wouldn't stand for it." Andrea smiled, feeling some of her anger dissipate. If she never had to talk to Margo Sloan again, it wouldn't be too soon. "I'll see you at the church later on. We need to go over those financial reports before the auditor comes."

"Pastor," Herb interrupted, "I just wanted to thank you for everything you've done."

She turned to shake his hand. "I know exactly how you feel, because I've been the recipient of a parish's kindness, too. It's a very humbling experience. Let us know if we can do anything else for you."

She said goodbye to the others and raced out to her car. Luke's admonition still rang loudly in her ears. If she hurried, she might just make it on time. For once, she'd love to surprise him.

As it turned out, she was only a few minutes late and joined the rest of the team for warm-ups. Other than darting her a lengthy glance, Luke didn't single her out, and a grueling practice ensued.

She decided Luke's coaching had definitely made the difference, because she no longer flinched when the ball flew at her. Better still, she'd learned how to punch it to the front line so it could be spiked over the net. Lisa, as well, had lost a lot of her fear and now made an attempt to return the ball instead of letting it fly past her. The tournament was only ten days away and thanks to Luke's help, it looked like they'd be ready.

The only sour note was Betsy Sloan's absence. She hadn't been to practice for the past week. No one talked about it, but Andrea knew it was Margo's doing, not Betsy's. The poor girl didn't have a chance with such a manipulative mother.

When Luke said everyone could go, Andrea locked the equipment in the hall closet and started for her office. He followed closely behind her and, when they were both inside, shut the door. She wished he hadn't done that. Being alone in the same room with him was no longer a good idea. "I only need a few minutes of your time, Pastor. I'm not about to pounce, so relax."

"I must have done something wrong at practice today," she teased, trying to ease the tension between them.

"Not as far as I could see. You're a fast learner and improving all the time. With each practice, you're becoming an 'awesome opponent.' That's a direct quote from Matt—who seems to worship the ground you walk on."

"It's a good thing you left Herb Wilson's apartment when you did. Otherwise Matt would have to reconsider his opinion of me."

His expression darkened. "Don't beat around the bush. Tell me what happened."

Andrea folded her arms and rested her hip against the desk. "I had a run-in with Margo Sloan. It became a slinging match of sorts."

"Over me."

"Luke, there's something you need to know. Margo has never accepted me as associate pastor. She doesn't think it's a woman's place and has shunned me from the day I was sent here. Any time she can find a way to point out my faults and humiliate me in front of the congregation, she'll do it. Up to now I've let it wash over me. But using you as a whipping boy in her battle against me is something else again, and I won't stand for it."

His hands clamped on her shoulders and he made her look him in the face. "In case you hadn't noticed—" his eyes flashed "—I'm a big boy and I can take care of myself. You're the one who needs protecting. If we weren't this close to the tournament, I'd get out of your life right now. But the kids are depending on me."

Was it true? Would he disappear from her life if it wasn't for the approaching tournament? And what about afterward, when the tournament was over?

"Do you think I told you any of this as a way of asking you to leave?" she cried, aghast, hardly aware she was clutching the front of his shirt. "The only reason I brought it up was to warn you to be careful in case Margo tries to cause trouble. I don't want you hurt. She had a look in her eye—"

"The only way she can hurt me is through you. I'll keep a low profile until the championship games. In fact, that's what I came in here to talk to you about."

"What are you getting at?" The pain in her heart was building.

"For the next week I'm not going to be available. Richie and I have already talked it over, and in my absence he's going to coach you as per my instructions. But I'll be back in time for at least three more practice sessions before the tournament begins."

She released his shirt. "Does this have any connection with your work?"

He seemed to hesitate. "No," he said quietly, shaking his head. His hands tightened briefly on her shoulders, then he backed away.

She sensed that his withdrawal was more emotional than physical. By not offering an explanation, he was effectively shutting her out, rejecting her. She told herself grimly that she should get used to this, but the pain she felt was nearly crippling. He would never know the amount of self-control it took to fight the tears and offer him a pleasant smile.

"The kids and I will try to practice everything you've taught us. Whatever you have to do, good luck."

"Andrea . . ."

"Yes?" She grabbed at the remotest chance he would talk to her, tell her what was going on.

"I'll see all of you in a week."

When he left her office, her heart seemed to shrivel. He had been on the verge of revealing something, she was sure of it, then he'd changed his mind. Why?

Andrea had often heard the expression "living in a vacuum." She'd never truly understood what it meant until she had to survive for a week without Luke. Her dissatisfaction with life, her emptiness, frightened her. Every time the phone rang at the office or at home, she expected to hear his voice, then reproached herself for hanging on to a dream that had no substance.

On the following Friday night, Andrea returned home from her hospital rounds and discovered Doris's car pulled up to the curb. Andrea parked directly behind her and they both got out of their vehicles at the same time.

"Doris. What a surprise! How long have you been waiting?"

"About an hour."

Andrea's face fell. "I'm so sorry. Why didn't you tell me before I left for the hospital? We could have set a time to meet."

"Because something came up after you left and I decided you needed to know about it, even if I had to wait until midnight."

Something to do with Luke? She instantly felt light-headed. "I-is it bad news?"

"Lucas Hastings isn't injured or dead, if that's what you're asking." Doris had read her mind with perfect clarity. "Let's go into your apartment and I'll tell you about it."

Mabel had her face pressed to the window as the two of them walked up the path. Andrea pretended not to see her and put her key into the lock to open the door. After turning on the living room lights she invited Doris to sit down.

"I think you're the one who needs a chair before you collapse."

"I can't. When I'm nervous I have to stand. Tell me what's going on."

Doris let out a sigh. "In a word, Margo Sloan."

"I might have guessed."

"Oh, Andrea. You don't know the half of it."

"She'd like to get rid of me."

"She's going to try," came the cryptic reply.

Andrea stopped pacing. "Tell me what you know."

"My source is a hundred percent reliable."

They stared at each other. "Betsy."

Doris nodded. "As you know, she sometimes baby-sits for me on Friday nights when Greg's out of town and Mom can't do it. Tonight when she came over, she was very upset and it didn't take much prodding to get her to tell me what was wrong."

"I know she was depressed when Margo made her leave the volleyball team."

"This is much worse, Andrea. Margo has filed a petition with the church headquarters to have you removed so you won't be able to serve in a ministry ever again."

"*What?*"

"Apparently she's been thinking about it for a long time. When you and Paul allowed Lucas Hastings to start coaching the kids, you put a sword in her hand. Don't ask me how she happened to be there, but she saw your car parked in Luke's driveway the other night and put two and two together.''

Andrea was too appalled to speak.

"One of the things she's accusing you of is gross negligence—planning a youth outing with an ex-convict, at the risk of the children's lives.''

"Does she realize she's indicting Paul at the same time?'' Andrea's fury was well and truly kindled.

"It's no secret that she thinks he's totally ineffectual as our minister and that you run the show. What she wants is a clean sweep.''

"Is nothing sacred to her?''

"I think the woman is demented. But she's dangerous, and she's operating on all fronts. She's gone straight to the Interdenominational Council to inform them that the man coaching our team has a prison record. She's trying to have him pulled out before the tournament.''

"I won't let her do that!''

"That's not the worst. She's asking for a full investigation into *your* background.''

Andrea froze in place. "She hates me that much?''

"Not you personally.''

"It's funny, isn't it? In the seminary, I always worried it would be a man who couldn't handle my being in the clergy. . . .'' Her voice trailed off, and she stared at Doris. "Is there anything else?''

Her friend nodded miserably. "Margo found out you went to the prison in Paul's place a few months ago. And through Mabel, she learned that you and Luke were on friendly terms at your adult group last month. She's using that to imply you were consorting with a prisoner long before he was released from the penitentiary."

"Consorting" was the right word. If Margo ever got hold of the prison guard who'd witnessed their embrace, she'd have a field day. "I'm surprised Betsy was so open."

"She's afraid, Andrea. She knows there's something wrong with her mother, and her father doesn't dare raise his voice to Margo. I wanted you to hear about this so you'd be prepared." Doris got to her feet and gave Andrea a supportive hug.

"All my life I've wanted a real friend, a person I could trust and confide in," said Andrea. "That person is you, Doris."

"What are you going to do?" Doris asked, wiping away a tear.

"Paul has been my spiritual adviser since I left the seminary. I'm going to discuss everything with him."

"Good. The sooner the better. Unless you need me to stay, I think I'd better get back home. Call me anytime, even in the middle of the night. I'll be over in a flash."

"You might be sorry you made that offer," Andrea murmured, then thanked her friend again and walked her to the door.

As soon as Doris left, Andrea hurried to the kitchen and called Paul. "Thank heaven you're in," she said the minute he answered the phone.

"Andrea?"

"Yes. We need to talk, Paul. Tonight, if possible."

"Right now is just fine. How can I help you?"

"This is going to take some time."

"We've got all night."

"Bless you," she whispered. Salty tears trickled down her cheeks. "Doris was waiting for me when I got home from my hospital rounds. It seems that when Betsy Sloan arrived at her house to baby-sit this evening, she...she unburdened herself and...and..." Deep gulping sobs overtook her.

"Andrea?" Paul sounded alarmed.

After getting herself under control, she launched into a full explanation, leaving out nothing that Paul needed to know. When she'd told him the whole story—including the fact that she was in love with Luke—she said, "I'm at such a loss, I can't decide what to do first."

"I'm not surprised, my dear, but I'm going to tell you something that should cheer your heart. I've weathered worse storms than this in my fifty-odd years of service. This, too, will pass. Remember that Margo Sloan had problems long before you arrived. Anyone who listens to her can't help but recognize that. And don't worry, no one's going to take her seriously."

Andrea drew a shuddering breath. "I hope you're right. My greatest fear is that she'll slander Luke. It isn't fair to him, particularly not after everything he's been through and the wonderful things he's done for the parish in the short time he's been here."

"That's true, and even if she actually goes so far as to petition the Interdenominational Council, they'll agree with you. Luke has paid for his crime. It's in the past and forgotten. Margo won't get anywhere. Trust me. She's the perfect example of a tempest in a teapot."

"Intellectually I believe you. Emotionally..."

"Emotionally she intimidates you," he answered for her. "Don't let her get to you. That's what she wants. Show her the stuff you're made of and fight her all the way. One day she'll grow tired of it and find a new crusade."

Long after Andrea had thanked him for his wise counsel and said good-night, she lay in bed pondering his admonition to stand up to Margo. That was exactly what she intended to do. Her love for Luke made any other considerations fade into insignificance.

He'd been gone five days—a lifetime. She wondered how she'd make it through the rest of the week until his return. She hoped the separation was just as hard on him....

CHAPTER EIGHT

ANDREA TOOK GREAT PAINS with her clothes and hair before leaving for church. She wore a dusky pink dress Luke hadn't seen before. The small pleats in the skirt, falling from the nipped-in waist, flattered her gently rounded figure. After a firm brushing, her hair gleamed and danced provocatively about her shoulders.

If there was the slightest chance Luke would be there today, she wanted to be a sight he'd never forget. Paul had told her to stand up to Margo. Andrea had taken his advice, but she was going to go even further. She wanted Lucas Hastings to fall so deeply in love with her that, despite all obstacles, he'd want her to be his life's companion.

Humming a silly tune, she went into the bathroom and skillfully applied eye makeup, blusher and pink lipstick. After dabbing on perfume, she fastened a strand of translucent pearls around her neck—a Christmas gift from Paul. They took on the color of the dress and brought out the pink frost in her lipstick.

Finally satisfied with her appearance, she left for the church at six-thirty, too excited and jittery to wait any longer. Luke knew she arrived long before anyone else on Sunday mornings, and she was hoping he'd be

there waiting for her. When she didn't see his BMW in
the parking lot, a sense of deflation swept over her.
But she refused to let it defeat her. The day had only
begun.

"Andrea!" Doris gasped when she entered the office shortly after nine and saw her standing in front of
the file cabinet. "Wow! What have you done to yourself? You're absolutely gorgeous! Stunning!"

Andrea reached out and laughingly hugged her
friend. "If you hadn't said that, I'd have had to go
home and start all over again."

"I guess you know Lucas Hastings doesn't stand a
chance."

"That's the idea."

Doris looked at her assessingly. "You know, I think
you fell in love with him at the trial."

Andrea smiled, her heart in her eyes. "I think I did,
too."

After a brief pause, Doris said slowly, "After the
other night I was afraid you might not even come in
today—and I wouldn't have blamed you."

Taking a deep breath, Andrea said, "That was the
other night. Today the whole world looks different."

"Because of Lucas Hastings?"

"Yes. And because Paul made me see that Margo
is a sick woman. No one will take her seriously."

Doris nodded. "I'm sure he's right."

A knock at the open door had them both turning
around. "Pastor?" Hal Neff stood there, staring in
undisguised fascination at Andrea. Her transforma-
tion must have been more startling than she'd supposed. He cleared his throat several times. "The

church council is convening after worship service to-day.''

''I didn't notice it on the agenda,'' Andrea stated in a businesslike tone, knowing full well what was coming. She exchanged a meaningful glance with Doris.

He shifted his weight from one foot to the other. ''Well, no.'' He cleared his throat, obviously flushed. ''A matter needing, uh, discussion came up after the weekly program was printed.''

''Thank you for telling me, Hal. I assume you've notified Paul.''

''I'm on my way to his office right now.''

''Good. Then I'll see you at the meeting.''

The second he'd closed the door, Doris burst out laughing. She quickly covered her mouth, but not before Andrea had joined her. She'd come a long way from Friday evening, and she delighted in her feelings of resolve and determination. She'd finally made some decisions—decisions that felt right.

But it was difficult to remain optimistic when it appeared that Luke wouldn't be showing up for services. Still, she refused to entertain the possibility that he'd decided to withdraw from the parish. She knew he was aware of the discord his presence had created; maybe, for the good of the parish... No, she wouldn't think about that.

In the middle of an interview with one of the Sunday-school teachers who was planning to go on vacation and needed to find a replacement, Andrea realized the council meeting had probably started. Apologizing, she excused herself. With a deep shuddering breath, she walked to the large conference room at the end of the hall, trying to keep her steps—and her mood—firm and confident.

She was halfway into the room before she sensed that something was different. Instinctively she scanned the fifteen or so occupants and stopped when her eyes met Luke's.

After a week's deprivation, the sight of the handsome face she'd studied for hour after hour in that courtroom was so thrilling she boldly returned his level gaze, uncaring of the others' speculations. His formal gray suit and tie were the perfect foil for his hair, which brushed the collar of his beautifully tailored jacket. Andrea experienced a quickening in her body just looking at him.

Hal's voice brought her back to an awareness of her surroundings. She took the closest available seat, across the room from Luke. But if it was any consolation, she didn't have to confront the glittering enmity on Margo Sloan's face.

"Now that Pastor Meyers is here, we can begin." Hal seemed to be having difficulty, because he kept clearing his throat. Andrea understood. He was not an aggressive man, and this was his first unpleasant duty as the new chairman of the council.

"I received a phone call from church headquarters the other day," he began. "Apparently one of our members wrote them a letter about a...problem. They sent the letter to me because they have a policy regarding such things. If I may quote, 'Local congregations are responsible for their own affairs, including how money is raised and spent, and how social issues are addressed.' So I've convened this meeting to air this grievance and—" he finished in a rush "—I'm

confident it can be solved to everyone's mutual satisfaction.''

Paul winked at Andrea. It warmed her heart, and
she had to bow her head so she wouldn't smile back.
The tempest had been put back in the teapot, just as
Paul had predicted.

''I have here a petition sponsored by Margo Sloan
of our parish council and signed by several members
of the congregation, including Mabel Jones, who is
also a member of our council. They are protesting
Lucas Hastings's position as volleyball coach because
of his prison record. They say they disapprove of an
ex-convict mixing with our youth in such an intimate
way. They feel he is not the right kind of role model
for our young people. They want him relieved of his
duties.''

He paused and looked directly at Margo Sloan.
''Have I left anything out?''

Margo stood up. ''Before this goes any further I'd
like to ask Mr. Hastings to leave the room.''

At that, Paul asked for the floor. With a pleasant
smile on his face he said, ''Perhaps you've forgotten
that all are welcome to attend this meeting, Margo.
When I found out the nature of the petition, I phoned
Mr. Hastings and asked him to join us. We've never
had a closed-door policy. You've brought serious
charges against a fellow human being. He has every
right to know where he stands.''

Andrea felt like flinging her arms around Paul and
kissing him.

''The circumstances in this case are quite different
from anything we've ever dealt with before,'' Margo
said loudly. ''We're talking about a man who stole two

million dollars for... for his own gratification. He's hardly the kind of person *we* want to associate with.''

Andrea couldn't remain quiet another second. She raised her hand, and when Hal acknowledged her she got to her feet. She could see the alarm in Luke's eyes and knew he didn't want her to be a part of this. His unselfishness only strengthened her resolve.

''It's a matter of public record that Mr. Hastings liquidated many of his assets to pay back the money before his case came to trial, which is why he's not still in prison serving a five-year sentence.''

She stopped for breath. ''I shouldn't have to remind anyone here that this meeting is not a court of law. Mr. Hastings has already faced a judge and spent time behind bars. I suppose by now you all know I was one of the jurors at Mr. Hastings's trial.''

Everyone nodded.

''Before he was sentenced, the judge asked him if he had anything to say.'' Her eyes sought Luke, who was staring at her as if he'd never seen her before. ''In a calm voice Mr. Hastings stated he wasn't guilty, and that in time he'd prove it.''

A swell of exclamations resounded among the group, but the only person she was aware of was Luke.

''For the record, last September I went out to Red Bluff in Paul's place and talked to Mr. Hastings for the first time. If any of you have ever been inside a prison, you'd understand that there *is* a hell on earth. Lucas Hastings could tell you all about it. Whether innocent or guilty in others' eyes, he has paid a price I pray no one in this room ever has to pay.

''And now I ask you, are we such perfect human beings that we have the right to judge and sentence

him a second time? And if so, for what crime? Shall
we list the charges? First of all, he's guilty of coming
to this church the first week he was released and asking if he could do volunteer work. Second, he's guilty
of shaping up our volleyball team so we actually have
a chance at the championship.

"The only time he didn't show up for practice was
when he was on the job, flying for his company. He
had to make an emergency landing and barely escaped with his life, then had to walk twenty miles
through forest for help."

Everyone gasped and made commiserating comments. "He's guilty of befriending Casey, who's
needed a firm hand for a long time. Let me see, what
else? Oh, he's guilty of donating the entire contents of
his study to Herb Wilson—without even being asked.
He's definitely guilty of providing the most exciting
youth outing this parish has ever seen, which he arranged at his own time and expense. How many of you
would give so many hours after being out of work for
six months?"

Pandemonium broke loose, and Andrea had to
work to raise her voice. "As associate pastor of this
parish, I'd like to put Mr. Hastings's worthiness to la-
bor among us to a vote. I'd also like to suggest that,
as it stands, this petition is slanderous and defaming.
Mr. Hastings would have every constitutional right to
hire an attorney and take his accuser to court."

Andrea sat down, her energy spent. To her astonishment, Margo rushed out of the room, a tragic figure who stirred Andrea's compassion in spite of
everything. Mabel, she noted, didn't follow.

"Does ... does anyone else wish to speak?" Hal stammered, clearly overwhelmed by Andrea's speech. Silence greeted his question. "All in favor of allowing Lucas Hastings to continue his work with the young people of our parish, raise your hands."

The vote of approbation brought a lump to Andrea's throat.

"All against?"

"Oh, for heaven's sake, Hal!" Mabel chastised. It struck Andrea as so funny that she started to laugh. At that point all the council members—including Mabel—were on their feet, shaking Luke's hand, clapping him on the shoulder, assuring him that they didn't take any stock in the petition. Judging from his reaction, he was genuinely touched by the outpouring of friendliness.

Paul made his way over to her and grasped her hands between his own. "Andrea, Andrea. You were magnificent today. In fact, you made me so proud this old ticker of mine got a real workout."

She immediately frowned. "Are you all right, Paul?"

He laughed and shook his head. "I've never been better. If I didn't know God wanted you here in this parish, I'd say you missed your calling as an attorney."

"And I'd say that if I didn't know God needed you to teach me about my pastorship, you missed your calling as a psychologist."

Misty-eyed, he patted her hands. "We make a good team, don't we?"

"The best!" Her voice trembled. "Paul, I'm worried about Margo."

"You took the words right out of my mouth. I'm going to drive over to her house today and talk to her."

"I'd like to do the same, but I know I wouldn't be welcome. In a few days I'll write her a letter. She'll probably tear it up, but I have to try. Good luck with Margo. And, Paul . . . thank you again from the bottom of my heart."

Once Paul had left the room, Andrea was in a quandary. She wanted to speak to Luke, but some of the men had engaged him in conversation. Realizing it might be a few minutes' wait, she decided to slip down the hall to her office for her coat and purse.

But no sooner had she taken a step out the door than her arm was caught from behind. Her heart leapt in her chest.

"Not so fast," he whispered. "I know you have your group meeting tonight, but you're going to have to cancel it because I've got other plans for us."

He'd said the words she was dying to hear. She raised a flushed face to him, her eyes quietly assessing his features for any changes since he'd been away. Surely Luke was aware of her heightened excitement; nothing seemed to escape his notice. "At morning service I announced that I was postponing the meeting until next week. As it turns out, I'm all yours. Just let me get my purse."

From the way his hand tightened on her forearm, she guessed that her capitulation was the last thing he'd expected. When it registered that she wasn't offering any resistance, he loosened his grip and walked her the short distance to her office.

He let her go so she could pull her bag from the bottom drawer of her desk. Then she straightened, looking him full in the face. Since entering her office, neither of them had said anything, and she was suddenly conscious of the unnatural quiet.

Obeying blind impulse, she confessed, "It's good to see you again, Luke."

He said something she couldn't quite catch and raked a hand through his hair, disheveling it. The tension between them was palpable. Her senses had come alive to everything about him. "Are you ready?" he asked tautly, holding out her coat.

"Yes." The word was a mere whisper.

"Let's go." He sounded almost breathless.

A cold wind disordered her hair as he walked her to his car. She'd forgotten about the low bucket seats and blushed when her dress rode up to her thighs as Luke helped her inside. His gaze lingered on her long slender legs; after witnessing her struggle to pull the hem over her knees, he shut the door.

While he went around to his side, she drew a shaky breath. The interior was filled with the scent of rich leather—and of Luke himself. He levered himself into the driver's seat and closed the door, but didn't start the engine.

Turning to her with a sober expression, he said, "Well, shall I do the right thing and let you go home in your own car, or shall we drive off into the sunset?"

The answer to that question was easy. Feeling slightly reckless, she replied simply, "The sunset."

His knuckles stood out white against the steering wheel. "Do you have any idea what you're saying?"

She spoke calmly. "If you've changed your mind about wanting to be with me, please say so."

"This isn't a game, Andrea." As if to emphasize the point, he placed his hand on her thigh. "If you come with me now, there's no going back."

Andrea didn't want to go back. She wanted to go forward. With Luke. As his wife. And she believed with all her heart that it was what he wanted, too. Even if she was a pastor.

"Are you asking me to go away on a vacation with you? Because if you are, the answer is yes. Other than your trial, I haven't taken a day off work for two years."

She heard his sharp intake of breath before he said, "The idea of going off someplace with you has been on my mind since the early days of the trial. But I'm not taking you away until the tournament and a few personal matters are behind me."

His admission was more than she'd hoped for. "Then what is it you're asking?"

He lifted his hand from her leg. "You know very well. I want you with me until I have to get up for work tomorrow morning."

She averted her eyes. "I want that, too, but it isn't possible. I...I need more from a relationship. And you must know I can't condone sex outside of marriage." She paused. "Maybe I'd better go home in my own car, after all."

Not waiting for a response, she started to open the passenger door, but he grasped her wrist. "I promise to have you home by midnight. Does that reassure you?" he asked almost angrily.

"I—I don't thi—"

"Don't worry about it!"

If there was tension before, it was positively crackling now. They both remained silent as he drove to his house. Andrea could only hope that she was right, that he wanted her with him because his emotions were as deeply involved as hers.

"You've been in New York all week!" she exclaimed when they entered his house and she saw his luggage in the foyer. The airline tags were clearly marked.

"That's right." He didn't look in her direction.

Obviously he had no intention of telling her what the trip had been about. Determined not to be discouraged, she turned imploring eyes to him. "Humor me tonight, and let me play house. Last time you only got turkey sandwiches. I want to make you a fabulous meal. Would you mind going to the store and getting some groceries? I'll make a list."

While he stood there watching her, she pulled the little notebook she always carried from her purse and wrote down the ingredients for crab quiche, Caesar salad and her favorite chocolate dessert.

"There." She handed it to him. "I assume you have flour and butter and eggs—the basics?" When he nodded she said, "I'll let you decide on anything else."

He surveyed the list, then eyed her speculatively. "There's some white wine on the shelf above the microwave. I like it chilled."

"So do I."

His head reared back. "I thought you didn't drink."

"When I go out for a special dinner, I sometimes splurge and enjoy a glass of wine with my meal. But that's not often these days because I'm saving every penny to buy a little house."

"And what is the going salary for a pastor these days?"

"Not enough." She laughed gently. "If I'd been concerned about making money, this was the last job I would have chosen."

His expression grew fierce. "You're damn good at it. So good, you had everyone at that meeting entranced this afternoon. If you told them to follow you off a cliff, they'd joyfully do your bidding and drop off, one by one, blessing you all the way to the bottom."

Andrea broke into full-bodied laughter, then stopped abruptly as he moved closer.

"You really were something," he whispered, running his hands up her arms as if he couldn't help himself.

At his touch, she swayed toward him. "I couldn't let Margo get rid of our star coach without a fight."

"The only reason I came to that meeting was to protect you. Instead, I discovered you staging a performance that would have given Clarence Darrow a run for his money. I actually had it in my heart to feel sorry for Margo Sloan."

Her smile faded. "I didn't like that part of it, either."

"She needed to be stopped, Andrea. For her own sake, if nothing else."

"I know."

His head came toward hers. She met him more than halfway in a long, deep, scorching kiss that was more sensuous and more moving than anything she'd ever experienced. She could hear his shallow breathing when he finally whispered, "Make yourself at home. I won't be long."

For several minutes, she stood in the same spot, fingers to her lips, trying to regain her composure. For so long he'd been her obsession; now he was her addiction. And they'd be spending the entire evening together! She felt as if she were floating inches above the ground.

First she searched for the wine and put it on ice. Then, with a little more investigating, she turned up enough ingredients to make the crust for the quiche. Might as well get that much ready before Luke returned.

Tying a large dish towel around her waist, she started rolling out the dough. Of course the phone *would* ring right then. She quickly rinsed her hands and reached for the nearby wall phone. "Hello?" she said before she realized she should probably have let it go unanswered. But it was too late now. She hoped that whoever was on the other end had no connection with the parish. She wasn't ashamed of being in Luke's home, but hated becoming the focus of gossip.

"Erin?" said a man's voice. "Hell, I'm sorry to intrude on your reunion with Luke. No wonder he hasn't phoned me yet. Unfortunately I have to talk to him now. This won't wait till morning. Put him on, will you?"

When Andrea could find her tongue she said, "He's not here but I'm expecting him shortly. If you'll give me your name and number, I'll have him call the minute he comes in."

"Hell, you're not Erin. I'm sorry. Look, tell him it's Chuck and I'm on my way over." Then she heard a click.

Like an automaton, Andrea replaced the receiver. With one phone call, the euphoria she'd been feeling had vanished. Her little plan to play house, to give Luke a small inkling of what married life could be like, had just blown up in her face.

When he walked into the kitchen a few minutes later, carrying two sacks of groceries, she still hadn't recovered from the blow. Because Luke had become her whole world, Andrea automatically assumed that when they weren't together, she filled his thoughts in the same way, to the exclusion of any other woman.

Before she spoke the words that would shatter their little romantic interlude, she needed to pretend for a minute longer that he was her husband, coming home to her at the end of the day.

No husband ever looked so good. He took off his jacket and tie, undid the buttons of his collar and rolled up his sleeves. Then he strolled toward her with a devilish gleam in his eyes, taking in her nylon-clad feet, the towel hugging her waist, her flushed face.

"Do you have any idea how sexy you look with that thing on?" Her heart began its ridiculous pounding as he drew closer. Nuzzling her neck, he murmured, "It makes me want to reach underneath and feel that gorgeous body you're trying to hide from me." Immediately his hands slid beneath the towel and over her hips and stomach in an excitingly intimate gesture. Her heart and body soared.

Then she bounced back to earth. At some point in time, she realized, Luke had probably said and done something similar to Erin. And he'd probably kissed her just as passionately. Earlier, when Andrea had inquired about the women in his life, Luke had denied any serious involvements. But perhaps he wasn't averse to having an affair with someone who didn't fall into the "serious" category.

In her naïveté, Andrea had foolishly presumed that he shared her values. And all because she'd been hoping for a miracle.... But maybe she'd had her quota of miracles. Maybe losing Luke was her ultimate test in life.

"Luke..." She spun around jerkily and backed away from him, trying to pretend her heart wasn't bleeding like an open wound. "I'm afraid we won't be having dinner, after all. You had an urgent call from someone named Chuck."

At the mention of the man's name, Luke's face, which had been alive with desire, darkened ominously. He swore violently. "What did he say? Something he said has completely changed you! What's wrong?"

"He said he was coming over. I assume he'll be here any second."

Luke frowned. "What else went on to cause such a drastic change in you?"

Now she'd done it! If she mentioned Erin's name, Luke would know her withdrawal was due to ungovernable jealousy. That was one human weakness she wanted to keep a secret from him.

"Nothing, except that he needed to see you at once."

"I don't buy that."

"I think you would if you'd heard the anxious tone of his voice. He said it was something that couldn't wait until morning. Why don't you run me home first, then you'll have some privacy."

His eyes were burning coals of fury. "Are you making the gesture for me or for yourself? We both know you're afraid to be alone with me, and now you're relieved that Chuck's provided you with an out this early in the game!"

When the doorbell rang, he looked, for a moment, like a man who was the sole survivor of an earthquake. But that moment was over so quickly Andrea didn't have time to blink.

Luke turned to her. "You're not going anywhere," he said in a menacing tone. Still clutching the towel he'd pulled from her body, he stormed out of the kitchen to answer the door.

Andrea stood there shaking. Her pathetic jealousy had roused the devil in Lucas Hastings.

CHAPTER NINE

WHILE ANDREA PUT things away in the refrigerator and cupboards, Luke reentered the kitchen, tossing the dish towel on the counter. She glanced up from her task and encountered the strangest look in his eyes. He no longer seemed angry, but she could no more read his expression than she could a tablet of Egyptian hieroglyphics.

"You were right, Andrea," he said softly. "Chuck had something of vital importance to tell me, and I'm afraid we're going to be meeting for the rest of the night. I'll run you to the church for your car."

With no more explanation than that, he waited while she slipped into her shoes, then ushered her out the back door to his car. They rode in silence all the way. He seemed remote, unreachable. Pain was exploding inside her as she got into her own car and headed for home, with him following.

For his own reasons, he hadn't chosen to introduce her to his visitor. When she reflected on her relationship with Luke, she realized he still kept her separate from the rest of his life. And he'd never told her he loved her. So she was deluding herself if she believed she could ever become anything as important to him as a wife.

Once she reached the apartment, they both got out of their cars and he walked her to the door. Andrea had already found her keys and opened the front door. The continued silence was so agonizing, her only thought was to get away from him as quickly as possible. And to stay away....

"Good night" was all she could manage before half running into her apartment. Thank heaven it was on the ground floor! To her shock, Luke shouldered his way past her and unexpectedly grasped her around the waist, lifting her high off the floor so she was looking down at him. His strength was astounding.

Gasping, Andrea reached for his solid upper arms to brace herself. "Luke!" Her mouth fell open in bewilderment. "What are you doing? Put me down. Chuck's waiting—"

"Chuck told me he called you Erin by mistake. Is that true?" Andrea felt her face go hot. "Is it?" He shook her gently and one of her shoes fell off.

"Whether he did or didn't doesn't matter. Please let me go."

His face, what little she could see of it through her cascading hair, grew implacable. "Until I have an answer, you'll stay up there."

"All right. Yes. He did mention her name."

"And as usual, you put two and two together and came up with a negative number. Now's your chance to question me about Erin."

"I'm not curious enough to question you."

"The hell you're not."

"Luke!" she cried again, exasperated. "Put me down."

"No way."

Her heart was fluttering like a frightened bird's. "I assume she's a woman you knew before you went to prison."

His eyes flickered. "That's right. What else do you want to know about her?"

Andrea tried to wriggle from his grasp but it was futile. "From the way Chuck spoke, I would imagine the two of you have been . . . intimate."

"Then you imagined wrong," he retorted. "She's the widow of the pilot I told you about, the one who showed up the last day of the trial. She's been calling me, trying to see me, ever since I got out of prison. Because she's so willing, Chuck thinks I'm taking advantage of the situation, but he's dead wrong. Do you believe that?"

"Only you and God know the truth," she stalled, but her heart was starting to thaw.

"Do you mean to tell me that the same woman who's believed in me all along can't see beyond her jealousy to trust me now?"

"Jealousy?" She practically choked getting the word out.

"If the shoe fits—"

"I'm not admitting anything!"

"That's fine with me. I could keep you in this position all night while I enjoy the view."

Andrea was fast losing the battle. "Okay, what do you want me to admit?"

"The simple truth will do."

"How would you like it if you thought I was involved with someone else at the same time I was seeing you?" she asked in desperation.

"Are you?"

"Luke!"

"You see, it's a little matter called trust."

"It's easy for you to trust me, because you know where I am, what I'm doing, who I'm seeing, every minute of the day and night," she told him. "Whereas I know next to nothing about you."

"Are you implying that you want to know more?"

"If I'd heard about Erin before tonight, then maybe I wouldn't be dangling in the air right now."

"I distinctly remember telling you all about her."

"But you didn't mention her name. She could have been one of any number of women."

"So now you're endowing me with remarkable sexual prowess. Hordes of females coming and going from my house. Your jealousy has definitely gotten out of hand."

"You don't have to rub it in. I'm quite aware of my flaws."

The obvious affection in his low laugh gave her new hope. "All right, Andrea, what else do you want to ask me? Now's your chance."

"Who's Chuck?"

"You mean you didn't recognize his voice?"

"Is he one of the men I met at the airport the other night?"

"Guess again."

"I can't." She was feeling the strain of being in this position. "I don't know anyone who knows you."

He lowered her until her feet touched the floor. With one arm still hugging her tightly against his chest, he smoothed her hair away from her face with his free hand. "Yes, you do," he whispered against her lips. "About three in the morning it will come to you.

Now I've got to go. Chuck's not a patient man. If I start kissing you the way you're begging me to, I might never make it back home tonight.''

"*I'm* begging...?'' Andrea countered, but when he let her go, she staggered forward and had to catch herself.

He reached for her and bestowed a chaste kiss on her forehead. ''Pastor, you want to take up where we left off as much as I do. But we'll both have to suffer until practice tomorrow.''

He was gone too quickly for her to tell him she was officiating at the marriage of Radie Ormsby's daughter, Bonnie, tomorrow afternoon. A dinner and reception at a hotel in downtown Albuquerque were to follow the ceremony. Andrea wouldn't be available for practice, let alone anything else.

IT WASN'T UNTIL just before the wedding the next day that Andrea unscrambled the riddle of Chuck's identity. Chuck was a nickname for Charles. Of course. Charles Rich, Luke's attorney. The wiry red-haired man who'd fought so valiantly on his client's behalf.

Something of monumental significance was going on. It couldn't be a coincidence that Chuck's phone call had come just after Luke's return from New York. More than anything in the world, Andrea wanted to relinquish her duties, run to the gym to find Luke and demand an explanation.

Instead, she had to contain her curiosity and prepare herself mentally to perform what she considered one of the most sacred ceremonies on earth. At the wedding's conclusion, Andrea left the chapel and went directly to her office to change out of her robe. A glum-looking Matt was standing outside waiting for her.

She invited him in and shut the door. "Hey, what's wrong? Why the long face?" she asked as she divested herself of her robe. "I expected to see a smile, what with the tournament only two days away."

"It's Casey. He didn't come to practice this afternoon. Luke went over to his house to see if there was a problem. But just a few minutes ago I saw their next-door neighbor, and he said that Casey's dad came into town this morning."

Andrea eyed Matt with concern. "He hasn't visited Casey in over a year. I can imagine how thrilled Casey must be to see him."

"Yeah." Matt pounded his fist into his palm. "The trouble is, whenever he comes around, it's only for a day, then he leaves again and Casey's all upset. This visit will put him off his game for sure."

Secretly Andrea agreed. Casey and Richie were by far the best players on the team. If Casey had an off night, the team would suffer, and she didn't even want to consider what would happen if he didn't show up. But family was far more important; certainly, no one could question Casey's need to spend as much time as possible with his father.

From what she understood, Casey's father had divorced his mother and moved to Washington state. Casey tried hard not to be affected by his father's absence. The man seemed to lack a fathering instinct, and on the surface Casey pretended it didn't matter. But Andrea more than most understood the instinct that drove Casey to yearn for his father, for his love. Her heart went out to him.

"I'm glad Luke went over there. If Casey's in a bad way, Luke's the perfect person for him to turn to."

Matt gazed at her shrewdly. "You're in love with him, aren't you?"

She could never lie to Matt. "Yes. Very much."

"Are you going to marry him?"

"Matt!"

His shoulders lifted. "What did I say wrong? Everybody's betting you'll be married before the end of the year."

Andrea bowed her head. She and Matt were too close for there to be anything but total honesty between them. And she'd done a great deal of thinking since last night. "There are a couple of problems with everyone's theory, Matt. For one thing, the lady hasn't been asked. For another, Luke isn't a member of the church."

He cocked his head. "Can't pastors marry outside the church?"

"Yes. But marriage is difficult at best. To start a life together with completely different philosophies would make it even harder. I'm a pastor, devoted to this parish. It would take a strong man to deal with that part of my life."

"Luke seems to be managing all right." He grinned.

Sadness tinged the smile she returned. "That's because when he was first released from prison, he was like a man on the loose, needing to belong somewhere until he could put the pieces of his life back together. He's doing that now." Her voice trailed off as images of his meeting with Chuck Rich filled her mind.

"Then you think he's going to move on one of these days?" There was alarm in his voice.

Andrea nodded slowly. The time for deceiving herself was over. "I'm sure of it."

"What will you do when he leaves?"

That was a question she couldn't answer.

"Matt, if you hear anything more about Casey, call me at home later tonight after I get back from Bonnie's wedding reception."

"Yeah, I will."

"And if I don't hear from you tonight, I'll see you at practice tomorrow. It'll be our last one."

"That's why we're not going to work out. Luke says it's more important to go over strategies and think positive."

"He was captain of his volleyball team in college. I would imagine he's got a few aces up his sleeve he'll pull out at the last minute."

Matt stood in the doorway. "I wish he'd stay in the parish for good. We've never had a leader who even compares with him."

"I agree," Andrea murmured. As she'd mused to herself the first day she'd seen him at the trial, Lucas Hastings was one of a kind. And he'd changed her life forever.

"Andy?" Matt whispered.

She looked up and saw compassion shining out of his eyes.

"I'm sorry if it doesn't work out between you and Luke. Personally, I think you two are perfect for each other."

He shouldn't have said that. The minute he left her office, she sobbed desolately, then had to repair her makeup before she could go out to her car.

The dinner and reception were lovely. Andrea and Paul circulated among the guests and chatted with the bride and groom. Andrea stayed as long as decency required, but she was anxious to get back home in case there was some word on Casey.

She hadn't been in her apartment five minutes before the phone rang. It was Luke. Her heart skittered all over the place.

"We missed you at practice today. The kids filled me in on your whereabouts. A wedding is as good an excuse as any to keep away from me," he said wryly. "Just make sure you're at practice tomorrow."

She sank onto the kitchen chair and rested her head against the wall in despair. She'd foolishly hoped he would want to see her tonight. "Matt told me you planned to give us a pep talk. He also told me Casey didn't show up. Did you find out anything more about him and the situation with his dad?"

After a brief pause he said, "Are you ready for this?"

"What?"

"His father's going on a rafting trip down the Colorado River this week. Out of the blue he asked Casey to go with him."

"Oh, Luke. That's wonderful!"

"Except that he's leaving in the morning. If Casey wants to go with him, he won't be able to play in the tournament."

She got to her feet and, clutching the receiver, started to pace. "Won't his dad wait a day?"

"Have you ever met the guy?"

"No."

She could hear his disgusted sigh over the line. "It's now or never. Just like that. Casey's in agony. He wants to go with his father. But he doesn't want to let the team down."

"How can his dad do this to him?"

"Too easily, I'm afraid. According to Casey's mother, this has been his pattern. He does what he wants, when he wants, and hang the cost."

"I wish to heaven there was something we could do."

"Maybe there is," he muttered, "depending on Casey's decision."

"Is there any question in your mind that he won't go on the trip?"

"I don't know. Casey isn't a child anymore. He's starting to see through his father. This time, he may choose not to jump through hoops for him."

"You sound as if you're speaking from personal experience."

"I am. I finally saw through my grandfather. And although I loved him, I wasn't blind to the selfish motives that governed the way he lived, motives I couldn't espouse or relate to."

Andrea already knew that about Luke. In all the ways that counted, he was one of the most unselfish men she'd ever met. "I'm thankful you're there for him, Luke. He needs someone like you very badly right now."

"What he needs is a full-time father."

"Why can't you ever accept a compliment graciously?" she asked crossly.

"Why do you care so much?" He turned the question back on her so quickly she was at a loss for words.

"I—I care about anyone who does something good, something to help other people, then persists in refusing credit for it. People should believe more in themselves."

"Thus speaks Pastor Meyers. I want to hear why *Andrea* cares so much."

Her hand gripped the receiver a little more tightly. "You talk as if I'm two different people. I'm not."

"So what you're saying is that you care about me the same way you care about everyone else in your flock."

"Of course I do."

"Does that mean that Ned Stevens, for example, has kissed you recently?"

Even over the phone, Luke had the power to make her blush. "That's not funny, Luke."

"I couldn't agree with you more," he said in unexpectedly solemn tones. "One more thing—after the tournament Wednesday, I want you to come home with me."

"For how long?" She'd finally dared to ask the question that had been torturing her. Depending on his answer, she knew what she had to do. Any relationship with Luke short of marriage was out of the question. If that was what he proposed—just an affair—she'd have no choice but to locate to a new parish, preferably in another state. She couldn't bear to stay in the same city with him. It would be too painful.

There was a slight pause. "For the whole damn night," he said testily.

With those words, he closed the door on her heart, forcing her to follow through with a plan that had been in the making for some time.

"Luke, I'm leaving town after the tournament." When he didn't say anything, she started to talk faster. "As I told you the day we flew to Santa Fe, I haven't had a real vacation in over two years."

"Then I'll come with you."

Andrea couldn't stand much more of this. "Th-that won't be possible." She struggled to stay calm.

"Why not?"

"Because this particular trip is a combination of business and pleasure."

"What am I supposed to make of that remark?"

She flinched from his anger. "I'm going on retreat with some other pastors from the Oakland area who are friends of mine."

"Where?"

"To Alaska."

"For how long, dammit?"

Her eyes closed in pain. "That all depends."

"Stop being cryptic, Andrea." It was on the tip of her tongue to remind him he'd never been anything else with her. But at this point, turning their conversation into an argument would solve nothing and conceivably make matters worse.

"I'm planning to relocate to another parish." That would be at least five years sooner than she'd originally anticipated.

After an interminable moment he said, "I thought the parish was your home."

"Only temporarily. The church expects us to relocate every so often. It renews us, revitalizes our commitment. I've served my apprenticeship here. Now there's an opportunity to work in an exciting new capacity. I'm going to check it out while I'm gone."

"It would have to be extraordinary to walk out on all the kids after only two years, not to mention Paul and an entire congregation of people who love you." He drove the knife so deeply and expertly, it drew blood. Tonight she'd have to sit down and write two letters of resignation. One to the congregation. The other to Paul....

"What's your hurry? And why this week?" His questions sounded like a repeating rifle.

"Because this particular opportunity doesn't come around very often, and I'll have to make a decision right away." The sooner the better. Fortunately her contract with the church required that she give only thirty days' notice. If she couldn't have Luke, then she needed to make a new life someplace else, away from even the slightest chance that they could run into each other.

"What opportunity could possibly offer you the same happiness you find right here in Albuquerque?"

"This one happens to be on the water."

"Pardon?"

She moistened her lips. "The pastorship is based on a boat that visits all the logging and fishing camps in remote areas of Alaska. The majority of the families who make up those camps rarely get to a big city more than once a year. So the parish goes to them. It's an innovative way to serve, and one that appeals to me."

She hardly recognized the voice that countered, "Those camps are also filled with men who have no ties and no qualms about jumping into bed with the first available woman. You'd have your work cut out in ways that would make the inmates at Red Bluff resemble a gathering of saints by comparison.''

She cleared her throat. ''If it was as bad as you say, the church wouldn't have a ministry there.''

''Something tells me I'm the reason you're prepared to make this leap to destruction. You've continually defended me to the world, but in the end I'll always be an ex-con, and that's the one bitter pill you can't swallow.''

''No, Luke!'' she cried frantically. ''I won't have you thinking that.'' In a split second she decided to blurt out the truth. Later, it would embarrass both of them, but right now that didn't seem to matter. ''If you must know the real reason, it's beca—''

''Save your platitudes for those who'll believe them,'' he interrupted brutally. ''Before you do anything so rash as to disrupt the tranquillity of an entire parish, let me assure you that once the volleyball tournament is over, I'll disappear from your life and leave you as inviolate as I found you. See you at practice . . . Pastor.''

A blackness descended on Andrea when she heard the click that literally and figuratively severed their connection.

CHAPTER TEN

"ANDY? I'VE BEEN ABLE to put everyone else off, but this time you have a visitor."

When she heard Doris's voice, Andrea lifted a wan face to her secretary. After spending a tortured night writing her resignation, she'd been hibernating in her office since early morning in the vain attempt to block the memory of last night's phone call from her mind. "Who is it? Do you know?"

Doris shook her head. "He preferred not to give his name. If you want me to tell him you're busy, just say so." Doris knew it was over between Andrea and Luke and had willingly run interference for her all day.

Andrea glanced at her watch through swollen eyelids. It was three-thirty and practice was at five. She still had a mountain of paperwork to process so Paul wouldn't be inundated when she left on her retreat Thursday.

"Give me two minutes to freshen up, then send him in. And Doris?" The blond woman paused in the doorway. "Thanks for everything."

Doris smiled in understanding and went back to her office while Andrea reached for her purse. She groaned when she saw her face in the glass of the framed scripture on her wall. Quickly she applied lipstick, then used some powder to hide her red nose. There was nothing she could do about her eyes. Her hair, which she'd arranged in a French braid, at least looked tidy. When she was playing ball, it was perfect. As for her clothes, she'd come to work dressed for practice, because she hadn't counted on seeing anyone other than Doris. She jerked around when she heard the gentle rap on the door.

"Pastor Meyers?"

"Yes. Come in." She put her purse back in the drawer and prepared to greet her visitor. When Charles Rich entered the room, Andrea couldn't prevent her slight gasp of surprise. Seeing him again brought back the memories of that ghastly trial.

He was dressed as if he'd just stepped out of the courtroom, and his wry smile seemed to reflect her own thoughts. "I'm sure I'm the last person you expected to see walk through that door," he began. "Will you forgive me for ever mistaking your voice for Erin's? Luke ripped me up one side and down the other for that blunder, and I don't blame him." His smile was replaced by a more serious expression. "I was afraid if I gave my name to your secretary, you'd refuse to see me, and I couldn't let that happen."

After such a sincere apology, Andrea could never have remained angry with him, even if she had harbored thoughts of blame. In his own way he was as charming as Luke. But why was he here? What did he want from her?

"It's all right, Mr. Rich. A perfectly understandable mistake."

"You're very gracious, Pastor. But it wasn't in the least understandable. I should never have jumped to conclusions where he and Erin are concerned. She's been in love with Luke for a long time, but Monday night he made it clear to me—he's made it clear to her, too—that he's never reciprocated her feelings. He'll give her his support and friendship, but that's as far as it goes. He also let me know in no uncertain terms that if my meddling did anything to hurt you, he'd never forgive me." Pursing his lips, he added, "I've known Luke a lot longer than you have, and I've learned from experience that he means what he says."

If only Charles knew how well Andrea had learned that lesson since the day she'd visited Luke in prison. "Mr. Rich, when he drove me home, Luke explained about Erin. Everything's fine. I'm sorry you took time out from your busy schedule to come all the way over to the church to apologize."

"I know very well that everything isn't fine, which is precisely why I came," he countered in his court-room voice. "Sit down, Pastor. I have something important to tell you."

Immediately Andrea's thoughts flew to Luke and her heart plummeted to her feet. "Something's happened to him, hasn't it?" she demanded. "Has he been in a plane accident?"

He studied her reaction for countless seconds. "When I left him at his house less than an hour ago, he seemed to be in about the same shape you're in."

Andrea was so relieved to hear Luke was alive the implications of Charles's remark didn't register until she'd subsided into her chair. Then embarrassment washed over her because she'd revealed so much of herself to the one man who was probably closest to Luke. "Please," she murmured when she'd composed herself a little, "sit down."

His lips quirked in amusement as he did so, reminding her once more of Luke. Nothing slipped by either of them. He sat forward, his hands clasped between his knees, staring at her so intently she almost felt she was on the witness stand.

"Luke says you're leaving town and that you'll be accepting a new pastorship someplace else."

In a voice devoid of animation she said, "I'm sorry, but I can't see what my plans have to do with your visit, Mr. Rich."

He sat back in the chair, his eyes probing hers. "Luke would kill me if he knew I was here, but I had to come. On Sunday morning, the news that Luke was framed and sent to prison for a crime committed by his two business partners will hit the media."

Andrea gazed at him incredulously while the miraculous news sank in. His broad smile attested to his own sense of satisfaction about the outcome of the case.

"*I knew it!*" she shouted joyfully. Forgetting everything else, she jumped from her seat and ran around the desk to hug Charles, who by this time had gotten to his feet. The minute she felt his arms go around her, she broke into sobs. "Somehow, in my heart, I knew it."

Standing on tiptoe, she kissed his cheek. "Thank you for all you've done for him," she said, unable to hold back the tears. "Do you know that while we were deliberating the verdict, I asked the other jurors to consider the possibility that his partners were lying? But they refused to believe the men would perjure themselves.'' She swallowed another sob. ''Luke must be so relieved, so happy.''

At her words his smile started to fade. Slowly he let go of her and pulled a handkerchief from his pocket to wipe her eyes. ''Oddly enough, he isn't. That's why I'm here.''

''I don't understand.''

''Now that I've witnessed your reaction, I'm not sure I do, either. According to Luke, you're running away because he has a prison record. But it doesn't make sense to me, when all along you've believed in his innocence. I'm going to meddle one more time and ask you the real reason you're planning to leave Albuquerque.''

Andrea hadn't expected to be questioned like this. She walked back to her desk to give herself time to think. She wasn't about to reveal the heart of her agony to Luke's close friend—her uncertainty about Luke's feelings and intentions, her belief that a marriage between an agnostic and an ordained minister couldn't possibly work.

''It's church policy that pastors relocate from time to time,'' she explained in a calm voice. ''An interesting assignment has come my way if I want to take it.'' She looked down at her feet. ''I know Luke thinks this is all because of his prison record, but nothing could be farther from the truth.''

After a quiet interval Charles said, ''I believe you, and I won't take up any more of your time. Good luck in your new endeavor. And may I say that I could have wished for eleven other jurors just like you at Luke's trial.''

No sooner had he left a shaken Andrea than Doris breezed into the room. "He's one nice-looking guy." She grinned. "And I'm not even partial to red hair. What did he want?"

Despite her personal pain, Andrea was so thrilled for Luke that she felt like shouting her news to the whole world.

"That's fantastic," Doris murmured when Andrea had told her. "But what's even more amazing is that you always believed in him. Any doubting Thomases are going to be sorely embarrassed when they hear that all along he was innocent. Andy, I realize you've been operating as if their opinions didn't matter. But we both know this will make a difference when you and Luke get married."

"Married..." Andrea paled. "I've already told you the reasons that isn't possible. It's over between Luke and me."

"Let me tell you something, Pastor," Doris said with calm authority. "I've learned an unforgettable lesson from you. Faith precedes the miracle. The water may still look murky, but give it a little more time and it's going to turn as crystal clear as a mountain stream. Do me a favor and don't plan to leave for Alaska until next week."

Andrea took a fortifying breath. "What difference is a few days going to make?"

"Why don't we wait until Monday, then you tell me," Doris replied. "By the way, there was a delivery a few minutes ago. A big carton, care of Pastor Meyers. Shall I open it?''

"Let's do it together.'' Knowing she wouldn't be able to concentrate on any more paperwork today, especially with practice about to begin, Andrea followed Doris to her office. "What's going on?'' she muttered as they pulled a stack of blue-and-white jerseys from the box. "At a meeting the other day, the council told us no uniforms would be issued because we don't have the funds. They said we'd have to make do with whatever we could find.''

"Which means you have an unknown benefactor.'' Doris winked. "You know, there's only one person who has the motive and the means to outfit the team with such gorgeous jerseys.''

Slowly Andrea nodded. Of course Doris was referring to Luke. Secretly Andrea had thought of him the second she caught sight of the jerseys. "The kids will be ecstatic,'' she murmured, loving Luke more than she'd ever thought possible for the man he was beneath that devil-may-care exterior.

"You'll do the entire parish proud wearing these.'' Doris's comment brought her back to the present. "I think everyone in the congregation plans to be there to cheer you on tomorrow morning. You *are* going to let me off work?''

"What do you think?'' Andrea smiled. "How about helping me distribute these?'' Gathering the jerseys in their arms, they headed for the gym. Everyone was there except Luke and Casey. Andrea had to hide her disappointment, but no one noticed her crestfallen face because all eyes were on the shirts.

Suddenly there were shrieks of delight and a mad scramble as the kids reached for them and traded them back and forth till the right sizes matched the right bodies. Doris smiled at her before returning to her office.

Eventually the kids crowded around Andrea to thank her, but she shook her head. "I had nothing to do with these. Your coach was the man responsible, and I wish he were here to give them out himself. But as long as he isn't, I have something else to tell you. Why don't you sit down for a minute."

Her serious tone produced the desired effect, because the gym immediately grew quiet. When they were seated, Andrea told them the news about Luke. The second the words were out of her mouth, their joy brought them to their feet, whooping and cheering.

"I know exactly how you feel," Andrea interjected. "So let's show Luke how much we appreciate everything he's done for us by playing our very best tomorrow. And if Casey decides to go with his father—" her eyes communicated with Matt's "—then we'll have to call on everything we've got and leave the rest to providence. Richie, until Luke gets here, you're in charge."

Practice resumed, but it wasn't long before Doris hurried back to the gym to inform Andrea that Barbara was at the hospital with her mother, who was undergoing her first session of chemotherapy. They wanted to know if the pastor could go up there and be on hand when the treatment was over.

Once again, Andrea asked for the team's attention and explained why she had to leave. If she didn't get back for the rest of practice, she told them, she'd see them at eight-thirty the next morning at Central High where the tournament would take place. Anyone who needed a ride could call her later. All the kids nodded soberly and sent their best wishes for Zina's recovery.

She went to her office and changed into a dress and shoes she kept in the closet for such contingencies. After putting on her collar, she threw on her coat, grabbed her purse and headed for her car. As she pulled out onto the main road, she happened to glance in her rearview mirror. She couldn't help but notice the jade green BMW turning into the parking lot.

Luke must have seen her car. The very fact that he didn't honk his horn or come after her, as he once would have done, underlined his intention to stay out of her life. More than anything, Andrea wanted to stop and tell him how overjoyed she was that he'd been cleared of the charges and to thank him for the jerseys. But by ignoring her, he'd made it emphatically clear he wanted nothing more to do with her. She pressed on the accelerator and sped toward the hospital, terrified that the pain would never go away. How would she be able to give comfort to anyone else when she was so badly in need of it herself?

"Barbara?" Andrea said when she saw her in the reception area. "I didn't think your mother was going to go through with the chemotherapy."

"I was surprised, too, but after Helen Sargent dropped by for a visit the other day, Mom changed her mind." Her eyes filled with tears. "You sent Helen, didn't you, Pastor?"

"Yes. Helen's been undergoing chemo for a while, and I thought she could reassure Zina."

"Well, your plan worked," she said, wiping her eyes with a tissue. "Thank you, Pastor. The doctor assures me she'll almost certainly go into remission with the treatments. This is going to save her life!" She gave Andrea a hug. "I hated disturbing you, but I know it'll mean a lot to Mom to see you as soon as she's through today."

The good news acted like a healing balm. For a little while, Andrea pushed her own problems to the back of her mind. Zina was delighted to see her, and she appeared in surprisingly good spirits despite her ordeal.

The three of them visited for half an hour or so in the waiting room, then Andrea walked them to Barbara's car. She promised to drop by their apartment soon for a long visit.

The minute Andrea got into her own car, she drove to Casey's house, but found no one at home. Then she went back to the church, thinking Luke might still be there with some of the team, but it was locked up tight. Changing quickly into her other clothes, she headed for her apartment with her game jersey in hand and phoned Matt. No one seemed to be home at his place, either. After calling the families of five other team members, Andrea discovered that none of the kids had come home from practice. Presumably Luke had gone somewhere with them.

Being left out of their pregame meeting compounded her misery. The phone rang a dozen times before she went to bed, and each time she thought it might be one of the kids, but all the calls concerned parish business. Except for Paul's. Apparently Doris had told him Luke's news, and Paul couldn't rest until he'd discussed it with Andrea.

"You knew in your heart that he wasn't guilty and you acted on those promptings to bring hope to an innocent man. And look at the result! Luke Hastings was given a new lease on life—and so was our volleyball team. I can't tell you how much I'm looking forward to tomorrow's tournament," he confided excitedly.

"But win or lose," he went on, "I thought you should know that in the team's honor, the welfare committee has been busy planning a dinner at the church for tomorrow night. I know you're leaving for Alaska the day after, but please plan to come. Stay long enough to watch the short program after dinner. It'll mean so much to everyone if you're there to enjoy it with us."

"I'll be there, Paul. Thank you." She couldn't manage to say anything more, for too many conflicting emotions were at war inside her, too much pain weighed her down. Paul would find her letters of resignation while she was on vacation. When she returned, she'd have to face him, as well as the congregation, and that was something she wasn't prepared to deal with quite yet.

"God bless you all. May the best team win."

Winning a game. If only everything were that simple, Andrea thought to herself as she got ready for bed. She seemed to be feeling regrets about a lot of "if onlys" tonight....

WHEN ANDREA ARRIVED at the high school the next morning, she immediately spotted Luke standing in line with the other coaches to sign in. His height, his lustrous brown hair and the solid blue T-shirt that matched the blue of their new jerseys made him hard to miss.

Her gaze reluctantly left him to survey the competition swarming the hallways, waiting for the tournament to begin. She could pick out her team in an instant because they were all wearing the distinctive blue-and-white jerseys—the best-looking uniforms in the building! As she silently counted them, her attention was diverted by a white-blond head. Casey's!

Andrea didn't know what to think, seeing him here. She walked over to tap him on one broad shoulder. When he turned around and saw her, he flashed a smile that transformed his features.

"Hi, Andy. Bet you thought I wasn't going to make it." The happiness glowing on his face left her more confused than ever.

"You shouldn't have stayed in town to play when you could've gone with your father. No game is worth that kind of personal sacrifice, Casey."

He tossed his head to get the hair off his forehead. "I knew Luke was counting on me and I couldn't let him down. Or the team."

"He wouldn't have wanted you to give up a trip with your dad."

"Yeah. I know. He told me. But I'd already made my decision. And do you know what he said?" Andrea watched in wonder as tears filled Casey's eyes. "He said, 'Tell your dad that the second the tournament's over I'll fly you to Moab, where the rafting trip starts, so you don't have to miss it.' He said it only takes an hour and a half. Can you believe that guy?'' He swallowed hard, obviously struggling for control.

Andrea had never loved Luke more than at that moment. Her eyes automatically scanned the area for him, but she couldn't see him now and assumed he'd gone into the gym with the rest of the team.

"When I told my dad about Luke's offer he went real quiet," Casey said. "I thought it meant he didn't want me to come along, after all. Instead, he said if Luke was willing to do that for his son, then he'd pay Luke for the fuel. He also told me he knew he'd been a bad father and that he'd been afraid to invite me on the river trip ahead of time for fear I'd turn him down." He sniffed. "From now on Dad says we're going to do a lot more things together—he wants me to come to Washington for vacations."

"Oh, Casey." Words couldn't express the depth of her emotion.

"He also said he would've given up the trip to watch me play except that his party needed him to help with preparations. Dad said he'd meet us at Redtail Aviation right there at Canyonlands Field at three this afternoon."

Andrea's heart was so full she asked Casey to excuse her, and she ran to the washroom. She splashed cold water on her face, then checked the elastic on her braid. It was another five minutes before she finally summoned enough courage to face Luke.

She walked briskly through the crowded hallways to the large gym, with its six volleyball courts. Central

High had been chosen because of its enormous seating capacity and its electronic scoreboard. The spectator turnout was even greater than Andrea had expected, and she felt her excitement begin to build.

In a glance she found Luke, already with the team, which had assembled on the floor and was volleying the ball around to warm up. As she hurried toward them, she heard a voice call her name. It was Paul, along with Doris and dozens of their parishioners, all of them waving madly. She smiled and waved back, then ran up to her team. Luke gave her a cool nod.

"So good of you to join us, Pastor," he muttered. "If you'd been at my house with the rest of the team last night, you'd know you're starting at the net next to Carla this first game."

Afraid the teenagers would notice his anger, she tried to respond as calmly and quietly as possible. "I had a hospital visit to make. When I got back to the church, you'd left and I had no idea where you were."

"If you'd ever come to practice on time you would have known we were going to watch volleyball videos at my house."

Fire blazed in her cheeks, and she began to say something biting in response, but an official blew the whistle signaling the start of the game. Luke took his place at the sidelines, and from then on Andrea channeled her pain and frustration into spiking the ball at every opportunity.

Andrea was only medium height, but with Luke's help she had learned how to get the most stretch from her jumps. For the first time, she truly relished getting a piece of the ball. Luke's anger seemed to give her a competitive edge she hadn't displayed at practice.

They won the first game hands down. But during the time-out while everyone geared up for the second round, Luke told them not to get too confident because it was still early in the day. Andrea listened attentively to his directions and suggestions but she refused to look at him.

They went into the second eight-minute round with a game plan, and though the competition was worthy, they obviously didn't have their strategies worked out. Andrea's team moved into the lead quickly. In an unguarded moment, she turned her head and caught Luke gazing at her with something akin to admiration in his eyes. She was so surprised, she forgot to pay attention to the game and missed the next ball, which cost them a point. But they still won the game.

Andrea was furious with herself for losing her concentration, and all because she'd wanted Luke's approval. She vowed to ignore him for the rest of the game, even if it killed her.

The third round went much like the first. The opposition hadn't put in the same kind of practice as Andrea's team and didn't have their moves synchronized. They were given a thorough trouncing. At time-out, everyone went out to the water fountain in the hall, and Paul followed. Grinning from ear to ear, he gave each team member a hug. Andrea wanted her team to win for him as much as for Luke.

After the fourth round, which wasn't as easy to win, they reached the semifinal match. Luke drew them into a huddle. "Listen carefully. I've been watching the team you're about to play. They're good but they have some weaknesses. So go out there and sock it to them.''

''We'll get 'em, coach,'' Richie affirmed, and they ran onto the court and took up their positions. Andrea started at the net again and, quickly ascertaining the opposing team's weaker links, managed to direct her spikes there. So did Matt, and between them they made a good number of points, which definitely contributed to their team's win. Matt flashed Andrea a cheeky grin. She returned it, but her joy in the moment was lost when Luke muttered near her ear, ''Don't get too cocky, Pastor. The team you're about to play hasn't lost a round, either, and as far as I can tell, they don't have any weak spots. You're going to have your work cut out.''

Andrea turned away. She was so hurt and angry, she didn't dare look at Luke, afraid she'd say something that would embarrass everyone.

''Okay, everybody.'' Luke called them into another huddle. ''This is it. What we've been working for, practicing for, day after day. Now's the time to put our 'speed' plan into action. We're not going to give the opposition time to think because you're going to return their volleys so fast they won't know what hit them. That means total, and I mean total, concentration on your part.'' Luke stared at Andrea as he said it. ''Any questions?''

They all shook their heads and filed onto the court for the last game. The whistle blew; the battle began. That was how Andrea described it to herself—a battle. The other team was playing fiercely, but after only

a few minutes it was clear that Andrea's team wanted
the championship more. Casey surpassed himself with
some spikes Andrea was sure could win him a place on
a college team. It was definitely Casey's game. He
stunned his opponents with the accuracy and speed of
his delivery and they couldn't hold out against him.

When the buzzer sounded, a roar went up from the
crowd. The team went a little crazy—they cried and
laughed and hugged and dragged Luke onto the floor.
Suddenly he was being carried around on the boys'
shoulders. Andrea stood there in a daze as she watched
Luke's dazzling smile, which was directed toward the
kids. Not in all the time she'd known him had she ever
seen his eyes and face glow like that.

"Now there's a sight to gladden any fair maiden's
heart," Doris whispered teasingly in Andrea's ear.
Andrea whirled around and hugged her. "Congratulations, Pastor. How are you holding up under so
many blessings?" she asked warmly. But when she saw
the haunted look in Andrea's eyes she said, "On second thought, don't answer that yet. There are still
more to come, I'm convinced of it."

"You never give up, do you?" Andrea answered in
a tremulous voice.

"Not when it's a sure thing." She gave her arm another squeeze. "See you tonight at the victory dinner."

Doris merged into the crowd just as the judges asked
everyone to be seated for the awards presentation. The
winner's trophy was a huge wood-and-gold affair,
which would grace the display case of any church foyer
magnificently.

The third, second and first runner-up ribbons were presented to the various teams, and they received enthusiastic applause. But when Andrea's parish team was declared the winner, there was a thunderous standing ovation. The official called the entire team, along with Luke and Paul, to the microphone. He introduced everyone by name, then presented Luke with the trophy. Andrea's heart filled to overflowing when Luke promptly handed it to Richie, who embraced Luke, then Casey, then all the members of the team. Everyone was ecstatic, showing their affection for Luke with grins and pats on the back.

Andrea had been studiously avoiding him up to now. But she couldn't prevent herself from gazing at the remarkable man who, despite his own personal hell, had pulled an assortment of less-than-confident teenagers together and made them work as a loving, loyal, cohesive unit.

When she realized he was staring straight at her, she was reminded of that day in the courtroom after the verdict had been delivered. The same look of anger and bafflement was in his dark eyes. Was the glint of pain she remembered there, too? She couldn't tell.

She quickly lowered her head and started shaking hands with the other pastors lined up to talk to her. She was kept busy accepting their compliments for some time. When she finally scanned the room to congratulate Casey and say goodbye to him, she discovered that he and Luke had already left the gym.

She hurried outside, but Luke's car was nowhere to be found. That meant they'd gone straight to the airport. Since it was already past noon, they'd have to hurry to get to Moab by three.

For the past half hour, she'd been riding high, but now that the tournament was over, Luke would be bowing out of her world. He always meant what he said.

The thought of a life without him gave her a sensation of falling into a great void. The emptiness terrified her.

ANDREA WALKED into the gymnasium of the church at ten past seven that evening. With each step she took, her black hair floated around her shoulders like a cloud.

Most of the group assembled had already served themselves from the delectable-looking smorgasbord, which had been prepared by the welfare committee. The trophy sat dead center for everyone to see. Victory banners hung from the rafters, and it seemed as though the entire congregation had turned out to celebrate.

Groups of teenagers and parents were clustered around Luke's table, vying for his attention. She said a silent prayer of thanks that he'd returned safely from Moab. With uncanny perception, he lifted his dark head at the precise moment she'd found him. From across the expanse, his gaze narrowed on her face. After tonight she'd never see him again, Andrea reminded herself, glad she'd taken pains with her appearance.

Earlier in the day, when she couldn't stand her own company a second longer, she'd gone out shopping.

She'd bought a sleeveless smoky blue silk dress with a
V-neck and pencil-slim skirt. It was dressier than anything she normally wore for church functions, but tonight was different. She felt an urgent need to make an
impact on Luke; at the same time, she had to present
a cool, elegant facade to the parish.

She was the first to break the unnerving contact and
started through the serving line. Paul had made a place
for her at his table. Once she'd filled her plate, she sat
down in the chair next to him, relieved that her back
was toward Luke. Relieved, too, that she was with
Paul, who would understand if she didn't want to
make small talk.

Andrea was mildly surprised when Hal Neff got up
to act as master of ceremonies for the program. He
cleared his throat, which resounded loudly through the
microphone and brought a wave of laughter from the
audience. Even Andrea wasn't immune, and she gig-
gled despite her heartache.

He went through the litany of thank-yous and congratulations, called on Paul to speak and asked for a
few words from the team captain.

As soon as Richie had finished speaking, Hal said,
"And now we'd like to hear from the man of the hour.
The man who made this night possible. Our coach and
friend, Luke Hastings. Come on up."

Tonight Luke was wearing a suit that nearly
matched the color of Andrea's dress. The blue-and-
silver striped tie gave him a more formal appearance
and suggested to Andrea that he had plans to meet a
woman after the dinner. At the mere thought of him

with anyone else, she was overwhelmed by a new wave of despair.

With his familiar easy grace, Luke approached Hal and took the mike from him. An expectant silence fell over the hall.

"I've played a lot of team sports in my life," he began, "and I've been in many exciting competitions, but today's victory surpasses them all. This parish has the finest group of young people anywhere. My congratulations go to them and their families for their faithful attendance at practice and their ability to follow the rules. They've come out *grand* champions, haven't they?"

The clapping took a long time to die down. "Regretfully Casey couldn't be with us tonight." A slow smile lifted the corner of his mouth. "But I have it on good authority that the Interdenominational Youth Council is planning a baseball competition for this fall, to take place right after the World Series. Casey told me to tell you that the next time we bring home the trophy, he'll be with us." Luke paused for a minute. "If you're willing to take a chance on me again, I'm offering my services as coach."

The shouts were deafening. One by one the kids jumped to their feet, stomping and yelling, "Yes! Yes!" until it became a chant. Soon everyone was standing. Andrea couldn't begin to figure out what was going on in Luke's mind, but she, too, stood up, feeling as if she was in some kind of trance.

Once the applause died down and everyone was seated again, she assumed Luke would return to his seat and leave the remainder of the program to Hal.

But things didn't quite work out that way. Luke's head turned in her direction and she felt the oddest sensation, a sort of prickling that ran from the top of her head to the tips of her toes.

"Hal made a mistake when he called me the man of the hour. Actually, the glory should go to the woman of the hour, my black-haired angel. That, by the way, is what I call Pastor Meyers."

Everyone burst into laughter and stared at Andrea, who blushed five shades of scarlet. "Those of you who were at the volleyball tournament this morning will agree with me that the description fits. She made miraculous things happen out on the floor and we couldn't have won without her."

More cheering ensued, and Paul patted her arm affectionately. Andrea didn't know where to look. She wished she could simply disappear.

"Not all of you know how the two of us met. I thought now would be a good time to tell you. It's very romantic, really. For each of those painful days during my trial, she sat with the other jurors and agonized with me as the damning evidence began to build. I felt her compassion, though we never spoke a word to each other.

"By the time she came to the prison, I'm ashamed to confess that I had about given up hope that there would be a life for me when my release finally came. I believed that the God I'd worshiped from childhood had forsaken me. Yet no sooner had I cursed him than Pastor Meyers made her appearance."

A profound stillness had taken hold of every person in the room. Andrea sat spellbound.

"The beautiful woman whose face and compassion had haunted my dreams since the trial was standing before me like a vision. For a minute I thought I must be dreaming. When she put her arms around me in what I can only call an act of mercy, I felt reborn. And I vowed I was going to survive prison and make the time that was given to me count." His voice throbbed with emotion.

"I also made a vow that I was going to win her love if it took the rest of my life."

Andrea moaned. Unconsciously she got to her feet, forgetting they had an audience.

"The rest you know. I came to the church and asked for a job, anything, so I could be near her. My plan worked, all right, and now I've reached the point of no return. Since Andrea told me that the parish is her family and that Paul is the father she never had, I thought I'd ask him right here, right now, in front of all of you, if I might have his permission to take Pastor Andy for my wife, to have and to hold, even unto death and beyond."

"Luke..." Andrea cried from her soul.

Paul got to his feet wearing a smile that couldn't be more joyful. He took Andrea's hand and held it. "Luke, I knew my Andy was in love with you when she came back from that trial. I never did tell her that I purposely arranged my trip to Japan when I did so she'd have to go to the prison in my place."

Andrea gasped and Luke flashed her a brilliant smile while Paul kept right on talking.

"I decided that if there was anything to those intuitive feelings of hers it wouldn't hurt to help fate along. Since that day it's been my earnest prayer that the two of you would eventually marry. Luke, when you showed up in my office after your release from prison, I knew that prayer had been answered. Lucas Hastings, you may marry Andrea Meyers with my blessing and, I'm sure, with the blessing of everyone assembled here."

The crowd started to clap, quietly at first, then louder till the din built to a crescendo, then slowly subsided. "Darling," Luke called to her, "come up to the microphone."

He'd never used that endearment before. Her heart racing, Andrea began the long walk toward him, but she was barely aware of the floor under her feet. When she was within touching distance he put a possessive arm around her waist and drew her close, smiling into her eyes.

"Now that Paul has given me his permission," he said, "you *have* to marry me." The crowd laughed and cheered. He sounded totally confident to them, but Andrea recognized a look of pleading and vulnerability in his dark eyes, a look she'd never seen there before. "Will this help?"

He reached in his shirt pocket, and the next thing she knew he pushed an exquisite diamond ring onto her third finger. With tears in his eyes he said the words Andrea had never thought to hear from him: "Intreat me not to leave thee, or to return from following after thee; for whither thou goest, I will go, and where thou lodgest, I will lodge; thy people shall be my people. Thy God, my God."

Andrea buried her face in his shoulder.

"Is that a yes or a no?" After such a moving moment, Luke's levity brought a burst of laughter from the crowd, and within seconds Luke and Andrea were besieged with well-wishers.

Doris was among the first to congratulate her. Hugging her hard, she whispered, "I told you the waters would clear. I'm here if you need help planning the wedding."

"Thank you," Andrea murmured emotionally. She would have said more but Hal had started talking.

"I know you two have a lot of planning to do, but keep in mind that this parish has needed a good youth leader for a long time."

"Amen." Paul brought up the rear.

Luke bit Andrea's earlobe gently. "What do you say, darling?"

She raised adoring eyes to him. "Is that what you'd like?"

His radiant smile made him look years younger. "I'd love it. My grandfather didn't believe in organized religion or youth groups. That's an area of my teenage years that passed me by completely."

Hal and Paul shook his hand to seal the bargain. When they turned to leave, Luke's arm slid to her shoulders. "I've been willing to share you—up to a point. Now I want you to myself. Let's go."

Without giving her a chance to comment he pulled her by the hand and worked his way through the exuberant throng to the door. "Where are you taking me?" She was soon out of breath trying to keep up with him as they hurried down the corridor.

"Someplace where we can be alone. Your office will do."

Her hand fumbled in her purse until she found her keys and inserted the right one into the lock. Luke took over from there. Once they'd entered her office, he locked the door and tossed her bag and keys onto the table. Then there was silence as their bodies and mouths found each other in the darkness. They started to make love with a ferocity that bespoke their long-suppressed desires. Andrea ran her hands and lips over his beloved face in wonder, wanting, needing to love this one man without cessation.

"All my life I've known something important was missing," she murmured feverishly against his lips. "A sort of emptiness, a longing for that perfect someone who had no face or name and always seemed to elude me. It was you, Luke. I took one look at you at the trial and that unseen part of me recognized you as my friend, my lover, my other self. Thank God Paul sent me to the prison in his place. I love you, Luke, and I'll devote my life to helping you forget your terrible ordeal."

Luke's response was to bury his face in her neck and cling to her, expressing more clearly than words his deep need. Andrea's soul seemed to soar beyond her body when she heard him say, "I'll always be thankful that my partners' greed sent me to prison. How else would I have met the woman created just for me? Even if it meant another five years behind bars, I'd willingly go through it again if I knew I could have you in the end. I love you, Andrea. I don't think you know how much."

He kissed her over and over again, deeply, almost savagely, igniting a primitive urge in her. When she thought of how close she'd come to losing him, her arms tightened around his neck and she shuddered involuntarily. Luke broke their passionate kiss long enough to ask what was wrong.

"I...I thought after tonight I'd never see you again," she replied. "I couldn't stand it, so I decided to go as far away as possible to try to forget."

Luke let out a sigh and gently kneaded her shoulders. "The way I acted during the tournament didn't help, did it? But you have to understand I was afraid you couldn't bring yourself to marry me." He paused, then said in a hoarse whisper, "Forgive me?"

"Oh, Luke, of course!" Andrea couldn't prevent the tears that sprang to her eyes.

"By the way," he said, and she could hear sudden laughter in his voice, "I've asked Doris to cancel your Alaska plans."

She went still. "When did you do that?"

"After Matt and I returned from flying Casey to Moab."

"Matt?" Her mind reeled at the implication.

He kissed her upturned mouth. "That's right. He didn't beg to go along with me just for the plane ride," Luke said wryly. "His real motive was to inform me that you were in love with me and that I'd better do something quick to prevent you from going to Alaska."

"He didn't!" Andrea cried, hugging Luke tighter.

"You haven't heard anything yet." He chuckled. "I then received a very thorough tongue-lashing about toying with your affections. He even demanded to know my intentions." Andrea groaned. "He said that if I loved you enough, then I should be willing to become an official member of the parish because it would make our married life a whole lot smoother."

"Oh, darling, no!"

He quieted her with another kiss that made the world recede for a time. "That's when I told him I already was."

"Oh, Luke..." Andrea hadn't thought she could be any happier. "When? You never told me."

"I asked Paul to keep it a secret."

"When I think how irreverent you were at the prison..."

"But you loved me anyway," he reminded her with mock arrogance.

"I couldn't seem to help myself."

"You have to understand something. I intended to wait until I could also tell you that I'd been exonerated." He wrapped her in a cocoonlike embrace. "When I asked you to marry me, I wanted to come to you as an equal."

"Is *that* the only reason you never told me you loved me?"

"Andrea, I wasn't about to saddle you of all people with an ex-convict for a husband—not until my name had been cleared."

"Lucas Hastings!" She rounded on him furiously. "Don't you know that never mattered to me?"

"After Chuck had been to see you, he told me the same thing. He said I was a demented idiot who deserved to stay locked up, because I hadn't taken what you were offering."

Andrea smiled. "I liked him."

"You'd blush if I told you what he said about you. It's a good thing he's a happily married man. After our honeymoon we'll invite him and Stacy over to our house for dinner. He's a crack poker player."

"I don't play poker anymore." But her mind was on their honeymoon and she started giving him kiss for kiss until her head swam.

"Just one more time?" Andrea could feel herself relenting. "I want to see the look on his face when the Pastor wins every hand. It'll serve him right after the lecture he gave me the other day."

"How can you say that when we owe him so much? This means you can be a stockbroker again."

"I could, but as I told you before, I no longer have any desire to pick up where I left off. When my partners were charged, the firm was dissolved. Now I'm considering forming a new investment firm with some other people, but I'll stay in the background, as an adviser. I'll do the same with Reynolds Air Freight. That way I'll be free to move when you have to relocate. Now that I'm marrying you, I want to spend as much time as possible helping you, being there for you.

"But after hours—" he nuzzled her neck "—I expect you to be there for me. I'd like us to spend all of your retreat in bed, starting right now. But considering that you're a pastor, I'll give you one week to marry me first. That's as long as my good intentions will last."

"Paul will help us," she murmured, her mind racing frantically with plans.

"That's good, because after your week is up, I'm going to do what I've dreamed of doing for more months than I care to remember. And you won't be able to stop me."

"I won't want to," she whispered.

EXACTLY ONE WEEK LATER, organ music filtered through the church to the foyer. Doris, dressed in emerald green taffeta, was Andrea's matron of honor. She turned to Andrea and handed her the bridal bouquet of white roses and gardenias. "Ready, Pastor?"

Andrea lifted the bouquet to inhale the heavenly fragrance. "You know I am," she murmured. "Aren't I shameful? I'm supposed to be nervous."

Doris grinned. "When a man loves you as much as Lucas Hastings does, you don't have a worry in the world."

Doris's four-year-old daughter, Cammie, dressed in an identical green dress with a garland of baby's breath in her blond hair, held the long lace veil that trailed behind Andrea. "Andy, you look so beautiful in my mommy's wedding dress. Like a fairy princess."

The dress was a dreamy confection of ivory *peau de soie* and alençon lace with small seed pearls sewn in the yoke and hem. Andrea turned slightly, and her glistening black hair brushed softly against her hot cheek. She smiled at the adorable little girl, hoping one day soon she and Luke would have their own son or daughter. "So do you, Cammie darling."

As the little girl beamed, Andrea heard the first notes of the wedding march.

Doris gave Andrea one last admiring look. "It's time."

"I know." Andrea swallowed hard. "It doesn't seem quite real yet. I haven't seen Luke since yesterday afternoon when he disappeared to make last-minute arrangements for our honeymoon. He's been keeping the location a secret."

"And I thought you weren't nervous." Doris smiled. "In a few minutes he'll be all yours, forever."

Forever. What a beautiful word.

Andrea watched as Doris, holding a bouquet of roses and baby's breath, entered the chapel and began pacing her steps to the music. Then with a nod to Cammie, Andrea began her walk down the aisle.

Friends of the bride and groom from near and far, and members of the congregation, young and old, filled the pews to overflowing. Everyone radiated smiles and whispered hushed comments as she passed. She'd made this walk many times before in her capacity as pastor, but never, not even in her dreams, had she imagined herself the bride. The magic of Luke's love had transformed her.

The moment their eyes met over the heads of the congregation, she felt as if all the joy and happiness in the entire world were contained in her heart. His steady gaze never left hers, drawing her toward him. He looked resplendent in his black tux with a white rose from her bouquet in the lapel, and it took great willpower for her not to run into his arms.

Before she'd even reached him, he stepped forward as if propelled by an unseen force. Clasping her hand, he pulled her against him, threading his fingers through hers in a gesture so intimate she could feel the beat of his heart. It was racing, like hers.

Andrea couldn't tear her gaze away from him. The expression of love on his face, in his eyes, promised her the world. She was scarcely aware of Paul inviting the congregation to be seated and welcoming them to this most sacred occasion.

In a husky voice she heard Paul say, "I love Pastor Andy as a colleague and as a friend. And because she's young enough to be my daughter, today I'm honored to act in the capacity of a father, giving away his child to a man we've all come to know and love."

He cleared his throat. "Luke, since you've already joined hands with Andrea, I take it you're anxious to become her husband as soon as possible." Luke's mouth curved into a smile, and the congregation tittered. Andrea felt herself flush.

When quiet reigned again, Paul eyed the two of them solemnly and began the age-old ceremony. After fervent pledges had been made and rings exchanged, Paul pronounced them husband and wife. "Luke, you may now kiss your beautiful bride."

Andrea trembled when she felt Luke's hands cup her face. He lowered his head and whispered against her lips, "I'm not making any promises, Mrs. Hastings, but I'll try to restrain myself in front of the congregation. I love you, Andrea."

Then his mouth was covering hers, stifling her own impassioned avowal. With so much love bursting to be showered on him, she could only show him what she was feeling.

A sigh of contentment rippled through the congregation, and all agreed they were glimpsing a little moment of heaven.